MURDER COMES TO TOWN
W.H. BESWICK

Once again, I have to dedicate my time to my talented editor, Meg Trast, who was more than an editor for this novel. Thank you, MEG.

CHAPTER 1

Jimmy Evans had been a lot of things. He had a handsome face with deep blue eyes and a winning smile. He was tall with a lean build that may have gotten a little soft, but all in all, he was a fine example of an American male a little past thirty. Riding a Harley Davidson Dovetail added to his "macho" image.

What he wasn't? He wasn't a nice guy. Life didn't give him bad breaks or a horrible family. Most people, except the young ladies who fell for his outward charms, accepted that Jimmy was born not evil but selfish. Apparently, early in life, he decided that the world owed him - not just a living but wealth and all that came with it. No one was sure where the attitude came from. His father was hardworking and well-respected in the small town of Digger's Cove.

Now, Digger's Cove was no New York or Beverly Hills. It wasn't even a city. It was one of those small towns that rarely appears on a national map but did occasionally pop up on a map of Oregon. On the other hand, it wasn't quite one of those blink-and-you-miss-it towns. There were two gas stations and two diners along the way, an excellent Chinese place for the locals. A new Mexican place had opened up and was becoming quite popular. There were rumors of a Pizza Hut opening, which was pretty exciting and gave the old men in the park something to talk about. - Aside from the debate about where the name Digger's Cove came from. There was no cove, as far anyone could find. There was a good-sized lake, which was good for fishing and such. Additionally, the name Digger couldn't be found on any of the town records. Most of the town's records were on paper, not on a computer, and went back more than a few centuries. There was always talk about putting it in a computer, but no one volunteered to do the work.

Maybe next year.

So, the name remained a mystery.

Changing the name had been considered but rejected as "too much work." Besides, Digger's Cove was a good name.

Don't get the impression that the people in the town are lazy. They didn't shy away from work, hard or light. They would get the job done. Changing the name would be inconvenient for everyone concerned. The town wasn't a tourist site. It only had a website a few years back. Some kids from high school set one up as a class project. Then, the Mayor had to hire someone to take over the site because kids, being kids, hinted that Big Foot and aliens were known to be in the area. That was the biggest excitement to happen in town for a while. A couple of those reality T.V. shows showed up, but, as expected, they didn't find Big Foot or aliens.

Most visitors just stumbled onto town when they made a wrong turn on the Five. They rarely stayed long enough to explore the town that seemed to be stuck in the past in small ways.

Yes, it was 2020, but you wouldn't know it. The houses on the tree-lined streets were built right after World War 2 or a decade later. Two- or three-bedroom houses that you rarely see nowadays. The lawns and flowerbeds were all well-kept. These were usually passed down from family to family, which meant you actually did know your neighbor - along with everyone else on your street.

The town was designed like a huge wheel. City Hall, the Sheriff's office, and the post office along Central Park sat in the middle. The streets then spiraled out like a pinwheel. Over the years, a few cross streets had been added, but the town remained largely unchanged in shape.

The illusion of the past was reinforced by the fact that no one in town drove a new car. The locals didn't like the new cars with their computers and other wonderful features. It was not that they didn't see the appeal of these features. The problem with new cars is that you can't work on them.

Hell, if you tried, you could lose your warranty.

Almost all the cars in town came from the forties, fifties, sixties, and seventies. Like the houses handed down through the generations, it was not uncommon to see a car parked in a driveway with the hood up and someone working on the engine. Usually, a small group of male onlookers stood around the car, offering advice and moral support while drinking beer. However, in the last few years, women have joined the onlookers. Some women worked on their cars themselves. Some men would watch with a beer in hand but only offer advice if asked.

Times were changing.

It was not unusual for someone to come to town and try to buy a car that had been in the family for years. The cars may have been old but kept in perfect condition. A few years back, a magazine had done an article on the city and its cars. Now, there was a car show once a year to raise funds for whatever charity was in need at the time. This was the big event, almost as big as the anniversary of Digger's Cove. The town brought in some carnival rides and such. Everyone had a good time.

There was much debate about when the town was actually founded, but a date was finally settled on so they could have the celebration. Some still complained.

Digger's Cove was a town the future left behind, which was fine with the locals.

Back to Jimmy.

Like most young people, Jimmy had left town. Not to seek his fortune but because he had put a local girl in that delicate position. His father did the right thing by grabbing his shotgun. Jimmy, knowing this, left town before the shotgun could be loaded. His father apologized to the family and vowed to do right by the girl. So, when the girl's parents died from the flu...

Everyone got their flu shot the following year.

Evans took the girl in and raised her and her son like his own.

Get the right idea; many young people left Digger's Cove. Some came back, but most didn't. In Jimmy's case, he would not be missed.

It had been five years since Jimmy left town. He mainly had drifted between Los Angeles and Las Vegas. The young man considered himself a gambling man. His luck reflected this as...not a reliable source of income. So Jimmy was forced to go from job to job, usually getting fired. Jimmy never fully understood the concept of working for a living. The simple idea is that you had to show up and work to get paid.

About a month ago, Jimmy was convinced his luck had changed. His boat, as they say, had come in.

The days of cheap motels and crummy food were over. If everything went according to plan, Jimmy would have all he would ever need.

Life - or God - seems to have a sense of irony.

Sadly, Jimmy had been wrong. His plan was no longer important. What was important was he needed to get home fast.

Very fast.

Jimmy was now riding the Harley that he had borrowed from a friend. Yes, the friend had been passed out drunk, and taking the bike without asking could be frowned upon. But in Jimmy's mind, it was the right thing to do. He had a mission in life. He would return the bike and throw his friend a few bucks.

It would all work out.

That was Jimmy's life motto. It was not a very good one if you think about it.

As mentioned, Jimmy's sudden desire to go home was a spur-of-the-moment decision. He had learned something so important that he borrowed the Harley, needing to get back to Digger's Cove.

Jimmy was thinking through his new plan. It wouldn't take long. A day, maybe two. For the first time, he would get it right. He looked up in time to see who was standing in the road. He had to skid to a stop. Confused and a little angry, he pulled off the helmet. Jimmy had a couple of questions. Then he saw the second person. He didn't see the gun, so it must have been a surprise when the bullets smashed into that handsome face.

It would be a closed coffin service.

CHAPTER 2

Abby Anderson stood before the mirror mounted on the back of her bedroom door. She was studying her thirty-two-year-old body, covered by a sports bra and panties. It wasn't really starting to show signs of age. Things were not drooping. She wasn't fat. Her belly was flat. Okay...she was a little soft. Far from her high school body. No way could she do splits. Of course, back then, she had worked out every day. She had been on the cheer squad and wanted to be homecoming queen.

She had lost to Becki Ryan, the girl with the biggest boobs in school and referred to as a good date. Becki was now married with four kids and no longer had her prom queen figure. Her fellow cheerleaders had all left town.

Abby had, too. Right after high school, she went to college, got her MBA, and never looked back. She moved to New York, got a great job, and was dating someone she thought was nice. Yes, back then, Abby thought she had it all. But in the back of her mind, she knew she was missing something.

Her father got cancer. The same lung cancer that had taken her mother. Both had been smokers, but never in front of her. Abby loved and respected her father. He had worked hard to make sure she got the life he felt she deserved. He had even visited her a couple of times in New York.

Didn't like it much, but did like the pizza.

Abby took a leave of absence from her high-paying job and came home. She took care of her father until he passed away in his sleep. It broke her heart that the most important man in her life was dead. The town saw this and tried to help her through her grieving. It was a loss to them, too.

Abby's father had been the Sheriff for thirty-five years.

It took time for her father to pass, so she had to resign her job. Abby understood this. She held an important position in the company;

it couldn't be left vacant...at least not for long. The medical bills piled up, so she sold her apartment to cover them. Went through her savings. Thank God her father had life insurance, so she was able to bury him with the honor and respect he deserved.

Since he had been a vet, an honor guard had been provided.

Her father had been town sheriff for thirty-five years. The new Sheriff, according to the local gossip, drank too much. This was proven not just to be gossip when he ran his car into the oldest and biggest oak tree in town.

The tree survived.

The Sheriff did not. He lived, but since he was born there, he was essentially run out of town for damaging the oak.

Abby, wanting only to help, took over the paperwork. To keep it up to date and help process the few arrests that were made. Mostly drunks and bringing in one of the Martin brothers. They had been feuding for ten years over the property line. Their father left them both half the farm. The problem was that their father had been vague on where to draw the line. A fight would break out every few months, usually at Eddie's Bar and Grill. One or both of the brothers would be brought in and locked up. Once they cooled off, they were turned loose.

Now.

Digger's Cove was a small town, which meant pretty much everyone knew each other's business. It was well-known that Abby had a degree and had taken some criminology classes. At the time, she took these for her amusement. More importantly, she had been a deputy during the summer vacations. It was also known that her fiancé had dumped her and taken her old, high-paying job.

Abby wanted to leave town but couldn't bring herself to leave. She was leaving Digger's Cove. New York might not be an option. It was warmer in Los Angeles. The movie business might be fun. She could get a loan from the bank and head back to New York or Los Angeles. Not that she really needed a loan. At this point, her entire life was back in the planning stages. She was just waiting for the new Sheriff to be elected, and she would be on her way. Like everyone else, she knew Willis Sawyer was not the man for the job. He had no experience in law enforcement, and he hadn't been born there. Willis probably knew all this, too, but he was thinking about the raise in pay and benefits.

Then fate, as it always does, played out most unexpectedly.

Abby, who hadn't even been running, was elected Sheriff. People just wrote in her name. Knowing the town thought they were helping her, Abby needed a real job, so they gave her a job. It paid well enough, had good benefits, and would look good on her resume.

That was three years and three raises ago.

"I really got to get out of this town," Abby said, turning away from them mirror. As Sheriff, she was supposed to wear a tan uniform. It made her look dumpy. She opted for jeans and the uniform shirt. The fact she always looked good in jeans probably had something to do with this fashion choice. Abby wore the badge but rarely carried a gun. She knew how to use it. Her father had taught her. She just didn't like carrying it.

After pulling her long, blonde hair into a wavy ponytail, she walked into the kitchen of her father's house, which was now hers. She needed another cup of coffee and breakfast. Not much of a cook, and not in the mood to try. Actually, Abbie couldn't boil water. She stopped at Bud's café for some bacon and eggs. The full pot on the automatic coffee maker made her smile. After dumping too much sugar and milk into her coffee, she gulped down the life-giving liquid. She closed her eyes, savored the moment, drained the cup, and poured another. Abby walked over to the window and looked out.

The FOR SALE sign was gone again. Abby had lost count of the number of signs that had been stolen. She needed to sell the house if she wanted to get out of Digger's Cove. Was the town conspiring to keep her here? The fact was, Abby didn't mind the job and was good at it.

It was just not New York or Los Angeles.

Then the phone rang.

Abby glanced at the phone hanging on the wall. It was just past seven. Who was calling? Everyone knew she wasn't a morning person. She snatched up the phone and snapped, "There better be a dead body for you to call me this early."

CHAPTER 3

There was a dead body.

Abby now wore a cap with the word Sheriff printed on the front and sunglasses. Not those mirror things a lot of cops wore. The glasses came from New York. Bright red frames with lenses so dark you couldn't see her eyes. She was standing over Jimmy's body with her hands on her hips, no gun to be seen. "Well," she said, "that is a dead body.

"What? You think I'd lie about this?" Bruce said. Bruce was one of her four deputies. Unlike Abby, he wore the uniform, starched, and pressed with a gun on his hip. His shoes gleamed, as did his badge. Abby always felt a little undressed when standing beside him. Well, all of her deputies, to be honest.

More to stop wearing jeans or sneakers.

Abby actually only needed three deputies but had four. She had been stuck with the Mayor's son. Her favor to the Mayor was turning into a pain in the ass. That was on her list of things to do today.

But now she had a dead body.

Bruce was a good foot taller than her - and broader. The deputy was not fat. He was big, having worked on a farm most of his life. He played football in high school and college but wasn't good enough for the pros. He came back and was hired as a deputy since his brother got the farm. Bruce had a baby face and red hair that always seemed messy. He wasn't the brightest guy, but he was smart enough to be a good deputy and loyal to Abby. Lastly, he liked working the graveyard.

"Never thought you were, Bruce," Abby said, squatting down and studying the dead body while avoiding looking at the face - or what was left of the face.

"So what do we do?" Bruce asked.

"Nothing. Murders are investigated by the state."

"So we're just going let the state take our murder?"

"It's not our murder. We don't have a homicide detective or crime lab. The state police do. They will lead the investigation. We will function only in an advisory capacity."

"That doesn't seem right," Bruce said, scratching his head.

"You have been watching too much T.V.," Abby said with a smile. "We leave this to the professionals. Right now, we know nothing about this guy. Well, except that he was a local who played high school football. He is probably a loser since he still wears his letterman jacket after all these years. He might be coming from Las Vegas. Skidded to stop for some reason and let someone shoot him in the face."

"What? How do you know that?" Bruce asked, staring down at his boss with a doubtful look. "You're just messing with me."

"No. Look," Abby said, pointing to the body. "It's all there. He's wearing a letterman jacket that has seen better days. It's blue and gold: Digger's Cove High School colors. We turn him over; I bet we will find the screaming eagle on the back of that jacket. You played football. He's got the pins on the front of the jacket. A pin for each year he played and lettered in football. You can see the skid mark. He stopped right here, and someone shot him. The bike didn't crash; it just fell over. One of his legs is still under the bike."

"Okay, okay, I see that. What about the Las Vegas thing?"

"The license plate on the bike is a Nevada plate. There is a sticker for a casino on the corner. At least, I am pretty sure it's a casino. 'Pots of Luck,' what else could it be. "

"Wow, Abby, you should be investigating this. That was impressive."

"Thanks, but the state cops get annoyed if a small-town sheriff sticks her pretty nose into their murder. Bruce, we are the amateurs here. When was the last murder committed in Digger's Cove?"

"December 1919. A little over a hundred years ago."

CHAPTER 4

Abby and Bruce turned to look at Walt Garner. A forty-two-year-old, twenty-year veteran of the state police. He was a thin man with a handsome face, but years of being a cop that came with seeing too much, drinking too much coffee, and late-night fast food had taken its toll. There were wrinkles around his blue eyes. Eyes that still sparkled, betraying that he wasn't completely burnt out and still had a sense of humor. He wore the same blue suit, white shirt, and red tie he'd always worn. Clean and pressed. Abby wondered if he just had a rack of them in his closet.

Walt stood beside Abby's police car, a 1955 Chevy Bel Air in perfect condition. The black-and-white paint job, along with the Police Department seal on the side door, gleamed. "I love coming here. You got some of the most beautiful cars."

"How you doing, Walt?" Abby said. "When you have finished drooling over my car, we got a body over here that might interest you. You may not drool over this, but it is a dead body."

"Good to see you too, Abby," Walt said, waving and shaking her hand. "You could sell that car and return to New York in style."

"Sadly, it is not mine to sell," she said with a smile. "Plus, it is a pain to drive."

"You don't like a stick?" he said, looking very interested.

"No, I like an automatic. A stick is a hassle. Driving shouldn't be a hassle."

"That's right, you had a Honda with all the bells and whistles. Why'd you sell that?"

"It wasn't a Honda, and you know that. It was a Lexus. It was a wonderful car, which no one in this town knew how to work on. I had to drive an hour to Cornwall to get it tuned up. Now, dead body. Look. So I can leave," Abby said.

"Why? You got someplace to go?" Walt asked.

"Yes, I would like to go get breakfast and then get back to my never-ending paperwork. I have a meeting with the Mayor."

"Busy day, but there is the body," Walt said, squatting down. "Obviously, he has been shot."

"Abby thinks he is local because of the letterman jacket," Bruce said, nodding toward his boss. "Thinks he stopped because of the skid mark. The guy just stopped and got himself shot. At least, that's what Abby thinks."

"Does she now?" Walt said, standing. "Oh yes, we got off track while discussing cars and breakfast. I looked it up. The last murder in this town was back in 1919. Just after World War 1 ended. One Billy Davis came home from the war to find out that his fiancé had married his best friend. She didn't even bother to write him a Dear John letter. So it was a complete and very unhappy surprise for Willie when he came home. His future life with her was all he had to cling to in the trenches. He was upset. So, using the pistol the army had issued to him, he shot his best friend. Didn't shoot her. Called the Sheriff and waited. He did go to prison. Only served ten years. He came back and married a local girl who had been writing to him. They lived happily ever after. The young lady who caused it all left town. Peer pressure. It can be a bitch."

"That was a nice story, Walt," Abby said with a dry smile. Her smile grew bigger when the coroner's van and a black SUV pulled up. "Oh goody, here come the lab boys and coroner. I officially turn the crime scene over to you."

"Not so fast, Abby," Walt said with a smile. "I am sorry to disrupt your busy schedule and breakfast, but this is a murder. I ran a check on the plate number you gave to me on the phone. The bike was reported stolen in Las Vegas. The good news? The owner knows who took his bike. This being a small town, I am hoping you know if this fella on the ground might be James Evans."

"That asshole?" Bruce said with a shake of his head. "If that's James Evans, someone did the world a favor."

CHAPTER 5

"Ah, sounds like he was a popular fella," Walt said with a shake of his head. "Now, him not being so well-liked may explain why he is lying dead on the ground."

"You know, the typical small-town bully and jerk," Abby said. "He was a couple of years ahead of me in school, but even I knew he was a jerk. He actually hit on me. My boyfriend at the time almost beat the crap out of him. I stopped him. Looking back, maybe I should have let him."

"He could catch and run with the ball," Bruce nodded.

"Those talents are only beneficial in certain social circles. Jimmy didn't play college ball," Abby said.

"Oh yeah, he did," Bruce said. "Played for one season. He got kicked off with low grades and just being him. Moved back here. Stayed here causing trouble until...well, you know."

"No, I don't know," Walt said. "Jimmy left town for a reason?"

"You can't tell it now, but Jimmy was a good-looking man with a certain charm," Abby said, looking down at the corpse. "He had a charm that worked on some of the ladies in town. One of the ladies ended up in the family way."

"He got a girl pregnant and didn't do the right thing," Walt said, pulling out a battered notebook and making a note. "Small town like this. I am guessing..."

"Walt, we are a small town," Abby snapped. "Everyone stepped up to help Lisa with little Jimmy after this loser left."

"The mother named her kid Jimmy?" Walt said, looking up.

"Family tradition," Bruce said. "Jimmy's dad was named Jimmy. So was the grandfather and...

"Thank you, Bruce. Walt gets the idea," Abby said. Lisa lives with Jimmy's dad. Her parents passed away a while back."

"Mr. Evans is the reason Jimmy left town," Bruce added.

"Threaten his own kid?" Walt asked with interest.

"Don't. Mr. Evans is the nicest guy you would want to meet," Abby said, stepping back as the coroner and lab techs came. They surrounded the body and began to work the crime scene.

Bruce moved closer. "But he is old-fashioned. If you believe the local gossip, Mr. Evans was going for his shotgun when Jimmy got out of town."

"Shotgun wedding?" Walt asked.

"Absolutely. Mr. Evans didn't want his grandson to be a bastard. Had nothing to do with Jimmy. The family honor had to be upheld and protected. This brings up the question: why was Jimmy coming back? His family or anyone in town would not welcome him back."

"So you are saying I have a town filled with suspects."

"That pretty much covers it," Abby said. She glanced back as another '55 Chevy black-and-white pulled up. A smile came to her lips. "Excellent. Here is my other deputy. I can send Bruce home. He has been up all night. I can leave Lucy here to observe."

"Lucy?" Walt asked, looking over as a short, thin woman with jet-black hair climbed out of the police car. Like her boss, she was wearing a police shirt and jeans. Unlike her boss, she had a holster strapped to her hip. She looked over and nodded. The deputy was a beautiful Native American woman.

"Hired her about a year ago," Abby said. "Stan Webber didn't work out. He was a little too enthusiastic with his ticket writing. People here don't like to get tickets."

"Wait, I got a ticket last time I was here."

"Well, yeah, you don't live here," Abby said with genuine surprise. "The speed trap is for out-of-towners, not locals."

"The mayor is good with that?"

"Yes, he got to keep his constituents happy."

"We got a dead body?" Lucy said, walking up. She was in her early twenties, with sharp cheekbones, full lips, and dark brown eyes that were almost black. Her long black hair was pulled back into a ponytail that fell to her waist. She glanced over at the body. "We know who it is?"

"Jimmy Evans," Abby said.

"Heard of him, but I didn't know him. From what I heard, it was better I didn't," Lucy said with a nod. "You want me to relieve Bruce?"

"Yeah, tell him he can go home. You stay here in an advisory capacity. Call if you need me."

"Abby, hold on, we got to talk," Walt said, studying the deputy. "Wait. Didn't I read something about you on the Internet?"

"It probably had to do with me being one of the last members of the Chetco tribe," Lucy said with a nod.

"I don't think I have heard of them. They're a real thing?"

"We are a thing. We may not be as popular as the Apache, Comanche, Navajo, or Sioux...but we are thing. Even though the government refuses to acknowledge us. They would like you to believe they were successful in wiping us out. They weren't. I will go relieve Bruce. Nice to meet you, sir."

Walt watched her walk off, then looked at Abby, thought, shook his head, and took Abby's arm. "Come on, we've got to talk," he said.

"I don't want to talk," Abby resisted a little but let him pull her away from the others.

CHAPTER 6

"I don't want to investigate a murder," Abby groaned, taking off her sunglasses and looking up at Walt. "That is your job."

"This is your town," Walt said, putting his hands on his hips and staring at the Sheriff. "I am an outsider. In this town, I am about as much an outsider as possible. They won't talk to me. I don't know these people. You do. And don't give me that crap about not being qualified. You helped out last year with that string of robberies. You led us right to the front door."

"That's because they turned out to be locals - and stupid," Abby said.

"Exactly. That dead body over there is a local. You're right; Jimmy stopped his bike. He knew his killer. His killer is a local, and you know it."

Abby put her hands on her hips, then began to pace back and forth, muttering to herself. She stopped and looked at Walt. "I am up for reelection."

"So?"

"I can't solve a murder."

"Yes, you can...wait a second. You don't want to solve this because it will get you re-elected. Abby, they are going to re-elect you no matter what you do. You won because they wrote your name on the ballot. Is anyone even running against you? Everyone in this town likes you. They will help you find this killer."

"Oh, crap. Crap! Crap!" Abby muttered. She stopped. "I just want to get back to New York or Los Angeles. I miss the big city."

"I've been to New York. The only people who like New York are New Yorkers. Three years, Abby. Do you really want to go back to New York?"

"You done here?" Abby said, sounding a little pissed. After a moment, she rolled her eyes. "Fine. We've got to go tell Mr. Evans his son is dead."

"You going to let me drive your police car?"

"Sure, I will let you play with the lights and siren."

CHAPTER 7

The Evans place was just outside of the city. Still in Digger's Creek, but it's a good hike on foot. A little over a thousand acres, it was considered a good-sized farm. The elder Evans still worked on some of the land, but mostly, he leased it out to his neighbors. The Evans homestead was a well-kept post-war bungalow with a porch across the front of the house. The slanted roof with dormer windows added to the charm of the home. The green paint and white trimming were not as bright as they once were, but repainting was still not needed. There was a small lawn and flowerbed with a large dirt area to the side of the house. Chickens, geese, and a couple ducks wandered and pecked around, not even looking up when the police car pulled up. Two more ducks swam around in a small pond just behind the house. They looked up at the arrival but then returned to whatever ducks do.

James Evans was sitting in a rocker on the front porch, rocking back and forth. He had the weathered look of a farmer, skin tanned and tough as leather. He was clean-shaven, with a full head of white hair. Wireless glasses rested on his hawk-like nose. He barely looked up when Abby and Walt approached. A large, curly-haired mutt of a dog looked up but quickly lost interest and went back to his nap. They stayed down the steps from the old man, looking up at him.

In Digger's Creek, you didn't step onto a man's porch unless asked.

"How you doing, Sheriff?" James asked with the smallest of smiles. "I figure you ain't here to ask for my vote. Which we both know you got. So it must be bad news. Just give it to me."

"I am sorry, Mr. Evans," Abby said, removing her cap and sunglasses. "Your son Jimmy is dead."

"I wish I could say I didn't see this coming, but I did. I am assuming it was not by natural causes."

"No sir; he was murdered just outside of town."

"Jimmy was coming back here?" James said. This made the old man lean forward, put his elbows on his knees, and look a bit surprised. "To Digger's Cove?"

"It appears that way."

"Excuse me, Mr. Evans," Walt said. "You don't appear to be very upset. I mean, Jimmy was your son."

"And you are, sir?" James said, studying Walt like a horse he was about to buy.

"This Walt Petersen," Abby said. "He is an investigator for the state. He will be leading the investigation into your son's murder." Abby nodded at Walt. "He's a good man. I've worked with him before."

"Oh yes, last year. You caught those Kilgore boys. Damn fools. Of course, they were never the brightest bulbs in the package. They could play ball, just not good enough for college. You going to be helping him, Abby?"

"Yes, she is," Walt said before Abby could open her mouth. "As a matter of fact, she will be taking the lead. I'm here just to help."

"I guess you are a good detective. You will need her help here." James said, leaning back. "Sheriff, you know how Jimmy was, and...how did you say he died?"

"Didn't say, sir," Abby said. "But he was shot. Riding a stolen motorcycle. It appears he knew his killer."

"And now you're here. So, it must have happened early this morning. I was in bed. Alone. So I got no alibi."

"Lisa wasn't here? Do you need an alibi?" Abby said with a big smile.

"Oh, Lisa was here, but she was asleep in her room, and little Jimmy was in his bed. He's got his own room now. So we need alibis. Could get a little sticky."

"Why would I suspect you?" Abby moved to the bottom step, smiling. "You still have that double-barrel shotgun?"

"Yes," James said with a laugh and leaned back in his rocker. "You can come up, Sheriff. You too, Mr. Petersen. I see you are going to suspect me when you find out what I made Jimmy do before he left town. I made him sign some legal papers before he left town. A marriage certificate, another of his legal rights as a parent..."

Abby said, "I thought you didn't find out about Lisa until after Jimmy left town."

"Oh please, Sheriff, you know me. I am no fool. I wasn't going to shoot him. Just made him think so. I let Jimmy leave town. He would have made a terrible father. Lisa and I will do a much better job of raising my grandson. A very responsible young lady. You know, she is taking classes over in Cornwall."

"Yeah, I heard," Abby said. "She's going to be a nurse. She is going to work for Doc Benson. She's at school now?"

"Sir, why would you want your son dead?" Walt asked, stepping into the conversation. "Only a suspect needs an alibi. You would need a motive to be a suspect. Since you and Lisa are doing such a fine job of raising—"

"Mr. Evans," Abby interrupted, "were some of those papers insurance policies?" She stepped onto the porch, looking down at the old man with another smile. "If so, how much?"

"Five hundred thousand, but I think there was a clause. If Jimmy died in a violent manner, like murder, it doubles."

CHAPTER 8

"Wow, one million dollars," Walt said. "I can see why you would need an alibi.

"Maybe so," Evans grinned and shook his head. "If I got all that money, which I don't."

"Lisa and Jimmy get the money," Abby nodded.

"Split right down the middle," Evans said, leaning back in the chair. "Lisa will get it the day she graduates, so that's a couple years off. The rest goes into a trust fund for Jimmy. He can get money for college but can't touch the lump sum until he is thirty. Young men can't be trusted with large sums of money. Jimmy seems smarter and has more common sense than his dad, but one can never be sure."

"No, one can't," Abby said. "See, what confuses me is why Jimmy was coming back. He won't be welcomed back with open arms. Well, then there is you and your shotgun."

"Was Jimmy killed with a shotgun?" Evans asked, showing nothing.

"Hard to tell. Most of Jimmy's face was gone. I guess it depends on what the shotgun was loaded with. Under the right circumstances, birdshot will kill someone."

"They will die slow. If you're going to kill someone with a shotgun, you are best to go with buckshot. Before you ask, I have both. You want to take my shotgun?"

"Not right now," Abby said, leaning back like she was trying to loosen her back. "I leave you to grieve for Jimmy. Oh yes, I need you and your shotgun to stay close. No sudden out-of-town trips."

"Sheriff, the only time I left this town was when I joined the army," Evans said with a small smile. "I wanted to see the world. The parts of the world I saw weren't worth seeing. It might have been nicer if there wasn't so much shooting and all those dead bodies."

"Yeah, war does tend to get messy," Abby agreed. "You tell Lisa I will be wanting to have a chat with her. I can come out here, or she knows where my office is."

"I see you are still not wearing your gun. Your father stopped wearing his the last few years. I guess Digger's Cove is getting more civilized."

"I have my doubts. You know, Jimmy's dead body up the road and all," Abby said. "You take care, Mr. Evans. We will talk again. Soon."

"Look forward to it." He said with a smile, just like a Cheshire cat.

"Yeah, I can see that."

Abby and Walt walked off the porch, heading for the car but stopping to look at the bright red 1965 Ford pickup parked in the driveway. She sauntered over to the truck and studied it for a moment. Walt came up beside her and nodded his approval. Abby stepped close and put her hand on the hood, giving it a closer look. She turned back and waved to Evans. "Love your truck. You go for a drive today?"

"No," Evans said, standing up and staring at her.

"Good talk," Abby said and headed to her squad car, shaking her head. Walt came up beside her. "You can drive."

"Thanks. What was that about?" Walt asked, going around to the driver's side of the patrol car.

"It's a cool day. Probably going to rain later," Abby said with a grin. "Mr. Evans just lied to me. The hood of his truck is warm. He went somewhere today. Be nice to know if Jimmy was killed with a shotgun."

"I'll find out."

CHAPTER 9

The first sheriff's station in Digger's Cove was made of wood. It burned down because the Sheriff at the time had a religious bend; he shut down the local brothel and saloon. Depending on who you ask, the Sheriff and his small congregation were run out of town, or well...

Let's just go with them being run out of town.

As Mr. Evans said, the town had become much more civilized. The brothel is now a very nice bed and breakfast.

When the station was finally rebuilt, it was made from whatever rocks and wood they could find. Not much thought was given to its outward appearance. It was a one-story building with one room and two cells, with bars on every window. The roof leaked, and the cell doors didn't lock right, so more than one prisoner escaped—not that they were that dangerous.

Usually drunks.

It wasn't this that made the township rebuild the Sheriff's station. It was considered the ugliest building in town. So until 1950, this basically stone-and-wood shack with bars stood by the city hall - a pretty, red brick building with nice white trim. It was mostly the ladies who demanded something be done. Rumor had it that most of the town's men had no problem with a jail with doors that didn't lock. But women tend to get their way.

One way or another.

They tore the shack down and replaced it with a one-story building, this time with a basement. Like city hall, it was made of bright red brick with a solid foundation. The only bars were on the cells in the basement and facing the alley. Can't have the depressed prisoners looking out onto Main Street.

Inside, on the top floor, were four rooms. A white-walled, open space with what had once been white tile. At some point, it was replaced with black tile. Easier to keep clean. A waist-high wooden railing ran across the room right before the front door. There was a swinging gate that could be locked. It rarely was because if someone really wanted to get in, they just had to jump over the low railing. The large room had five desks set up around the room. One for each deputy. There were three doors: one to Abby's office, one to the locker room and bathroom, and one to the supply closet. A staircase led to the basement where the cells were.

Paige Walton sat at a desk by the railing. She was the person who decided if you could see the Sheriff or one of the deputies. Paige was the Sheriff's clerk and dispatcher. A radio had been set up on a table behind her desk.

Paige was twenty-seven and considered very attractive by many of the young men in town. It had not gone unnoticed she tended to wear tight sweaters and skirts. Her blonde hair pinned into a tight bun and black frame glasses on her nose added to whatever silly fantasy men had about women. The people of Digger's Cove forgave Paige for the tightness of her clothes because she was a widow. A widow whose husband had heroically died in combat, saving several of his men. This left her with some medals and not much else. The fact she had been adopted also played on the town's sympathies. People knew, in time, she would grow out of this sexy secretary phase.

Paige glanced out the window and watched the Sheriff's car pull up. She stood up and went over to the coffee machine on a table across the room. The young lady made coffee with milk and sugar, moved to the center of the room, and waited. Abby came in, stopped, and looked at an empty desk set up in one corner. It was cluttered with papers, empty cups, and a stack of magazines. She let off a disgusted sigh and moved forward. She took the cup Paige offered and smiled. "You are a goddess."

"Thank you," Paige said. "Could I have a raise?"

"I just gave you a raise," Abby said, moving toward a door across the room with Sheriff printed on the pebbled glass. Paige followed along.

It was a small office, where most of the space was occupied by the old oak desk and office chair that looked brand new. Its newness hardly fit the cluttered office. Two wooden chairs sat in front of it. Two file cabinets were pushed against the back wall. One window gave her an excellent view of the brick wall of City Hall right next door. Abby went behind her desk, pulled out a bottom drawer, sat down, put her feet in it, leaned back in her chair, sipped her coffee, and took off her sunglasses and cap. "You were saying?"

"Raise."

"Oh, we are still on that. Can't. You're earning more than my deputies. And you don't even patrol or wear a gun."

"You don't wear a gun either."

"But I got one and know how to use it."

"I know how to use a gun. A lot better than Foster."

"Where is Foster? Out for lunch?"

"He still hasn't made it in. No raise?"

"Paige, I can't. I know. Why don't you go to the Mayor's office in that cute sweater and skirt and ask him for a raise."

"The Mayor's niece is his secretary. She wouldn't let me get close to him. Not that I am that desperate. I just need more money."

"Why?"

"Inflation, bills, mad money."

"The only way I could raise you is to promote you. What do I promote you to? Office manager? Desk Sergeant? The Mayor and city council aren't going to buy that, and they like you."

"Abby, please," Paige said, leaning into one of the chairs. I like to go shopping."

"You're serious," Abby said, looking over with raised eyebrows. She closed her eyes and thought. They both looked over when a young man walked into the office. He was wearing shorts and a baggy tee shirt. The newcomer was more chunky than fat. His hair was messy, hanging down to his shoulders. He slumped into one of the chairs and took a look sip on the drink he held in his hand. Then belched.

Abby rubbed her face with both hands and let off a long, angry sigh. She looked at Paige. "Lucky man, I left my gun in the lockbox in my car."

"Liar. It's in the bottom drawer of your desk."

"Yes, it is," Abby said, looking over her shoulder at the bottom of her desk. "Tempting, but this is the last straw. Mayor's son or not. Foster is out of here."

"Wait," Paige said, looking excited. "If you fire him, you will have an opening for a deputy. I have seniority over everyone. You could make me a deputy...better, Head Deputy."

"Head Deputy?" Abby sat up and leaned forward, putting her elbows on her desk. "First, I don't have a Head Deputy. Even if I did, you would have to wear a uniform. Do patrols. Write tickets. All that police stuff. Plus, I would have to get a whole new person for everything you do so amazingly well. Who would make the coffee? That was a huge deal in me hiring you."

"My cousin Shaun makes much better coffee," Paige said.

"I don't know your cousin Shaun. Is he new in town?"

"No, it's my cousin Rocky. He came back here two years ago. While he was in Los Angeles, his name was changed to Shaun. He thinks it suits his new lifestyle. Shaun got tired of Los Angeles and came back. Everyone in the family and friends has been very supportive. It is because of that show on Netflix.

"Let me get this straight in my head," Abby said, taking a long sip of her coffee. "You want me to fire the mayor's son."

"You going to fire him anyway. You can't put that on me."

"Make you a deputy, then give you a rank that really doesn't exist, which would include a raise. Then hire your cousin, who is one of three...no, no, one of six gays in our town."

"You don't want to hire him because he is gay? I had no idea that you were like that."

Really?" Abby snapped.

"Sorry. Misspoke," Paige said, looking a little sorry.

"I am thinking big picture. Mayor. City council. Today is just not the day to hit me with all this."

"Because of the murder?"

"Yes. The state police have dumped it on me. Saying this is my town and my people. Made worse by the fact the victim was Jimmy Evans."

"I didn't know him that well. My sister did. Said he was a jerk. But wait, I can help you with that. Born and raised here."

"I was too. Plus, I am not sure how Lucy will feel about it," Abby said. "Bruce won't care. He is happy working the graveyard. Phil won't want the responsibility. Still working on that novel."

"Feel about what?" Lucy asked, walking into the office.

"I'm considering making Paige Head Deputy," Abby said, leaning back and putting her feet in the bottom drawer again. "Right after I fire Foster."

"Could you do that soon?" Lucy asked, looking out at Foster, who now had headphones on. He was nodding his head while he read a magazine with a naked woman on the cover. "I am pretty sure he hasn't showered for a while. On the other matter, I am cool with that. Remember when my review comes up, and you're working out how much of a raise to give me."

"Everyone wants raises," Abby said, looking at the two women. "I want a raise."

"You want to be back in New York," Paige said. "So, are we doing this or not?"

"We? We? There is no we in this. It is me. The Mayor is going to be pissed at me. He might fire me and make one of you become Sheriff."

"The Mayor can't fire you. You are an elected official," Paige said with a smug grin.

"Sure, rain on my parade," Abby said, standing up and heading for the door. She stopped. "You two coming, or are you going to cower in here?"

"Oh, I am coming," Paige said, jumping up.

"I better since I am the only one wearing a gun," Lucy said.

Abby stopped outside the office and slumped. Foster was now leaning back with his feet on his desk. It looked like he was taking a nap. Abby stepped forward and stopped. "Oh God."

CHAPTER 10

"Told you," Lucy said. "He hasn't showered.

"Right." Abby walked over to the desk, looking down at the sleeping man. Finally, she pushed his feet off the desk. Foster started to fall out of his chair. He tried to catch himself but ended up on the floor. He jumped up, looking pissed.

"Hey! What the hell, Abby?" Foster yelled, looking down at the shorter woman.

"I told you to get your hair cut! Where the hell is your uniform?" Abby yelled so loudly that the young man jumped back.

"The uniform is uncomfortable," he said. "It makes me look fat. I figured I may as well be comfortable."

"Comfortable?" Abby asked, shaking her head. "You're not supposed to be sleeping. You're supposed to be out on patrol. Ellen tells me you didn't show up at the school. She had to act as crossing guard."

"They don't need a crossing guard," Foster said. "Those kids walk all over town..."

"No. No! Part of your job is crossing guard," Abby snarled. "No. It was your job. You're fired. Get out of my station."

"You can't fire me! I was appointed by the Mayor. Only he can fire me, so I can pretty much do what I want, or my dad - the Mayor - will fire your ass. Probably make me Sheriff."

"Did I just hear you just threaten the sheriff?" David Kelton asked as he walked into the station. He was a tall, good-looking man in his fifties, with blonde hair cut short to fit his face, blue eyes, and a square jaw. The square, wire-rimmed glasses on his nose actually worked for him. His gray suit, white shirt, and tie with ducks gave him the look of a mayor. He pushed through the gate and walked toward his son but stopped a couple feet away. "My God! What is that smell?"

"The lack of bathing for a few days with traces of pot," Lucy said in a deadpan voice. "Maybe beer, too."

"Hey, pot's legal in this state," Foster said.

"What is wrong with you? I know your mother didn't drop you on your head," David said, keeping his distance from his son. "Thank God she isn't here to see this."

"How is Ellen?" Abby asked.

"Great. Loves Florida," the Mayor said, giving her a smile. "You know, getting divorced was the smartest thing we ever did. We are much better friends now. I may go down there for vacation."

"Lucky you," Paige said. "I would love to go to Florida."

They just smiled at each other. Abby and Lucy rolled their eyes. Foster groaned and snapped, "Dad, she just fired me!"

David returned his attention to his son. "I give up. I am done with you. This is the third job I have arranged for you. No more. And I do mean no more. No more money. No more letting you live for free in your grandparents' house..."

"Probably have to have it fumigated," Lucy said. Everyone turned to look at her. "Just saying."

The Mayor chuckled and turned back to his son. "I want you out of the house by the end of the week. Keys."

"What...you want the keys to my car?" Foster asked in shock.

"It is not your car. It was your grandfather's. Don't think I noticed the scratches and dents in the fenders? You should have more respect for a 1955 Corvette. It's a work of art. I don't know where I am going to get it fixed." He turned to Abby. "You know, Henry is retiring. George is good for tune-ups and such, but Henry's the man you want for bodywork."

"No arguing with you, Mayor," Abby nodded. "The man is an artist."

"You going to give me the keys?" The Mayor turned back to his son.

"No, it's my car!" Foster said, stepping back.

"Sheriff, can you arrest him for stealing my car now, or do you have to wait for him to drive off?"

"Oh, that is a grey area," Abby said. "We probably would have to wait."

"But Sheriff, knowing what we know about Foster," Paige said with a smile, "he will probably make a run for it. That could be considered a possible danger to the citizens."

"I say arrest him now," Lucy said, pulling out her handcuffs. "No one will care because no one likes him. Oh, sorry, Mayor."

"No, you're right," David said with a smile. "Arrest him. You got showers downstairs."

"Soap and shampoo," Abby said with a smile. For the first time today, she was enjoying herself. "Deputy, arrest him."

"NO! NO!" Foster cried, sounding more like a baby than a grown man. He looked around and muttered a curse before pulling the keys out of his pocket. He threw them down on the floor and snarled. "I'm out of here. Anyone who tries to stop me will get hurt."

Lucy moved right in front of Foster with her hands on her hips. The handcuffs dangled down. Her eyes looked right into the young man's eyes. "Sheriff?"

"Mayor?" Abby asked.

"Let him go," the Mayor said. "I assume none of you wants to see him naked."

"We would just stick him under the shower, clothes and all," Abby said. "Go on, Foster."

"Fine. I would have kicked your ass," Foster said, looking into Lucy's dark eyes. She stepped forward. He jumped back, bringing his hands up to his face. "No, don't hit me!"

Lucy patted his belly and said. "I would hit you in this soft belly first. You heard the Sheriff. Git."

Foster rushed out of the station.

Abby looked at Lucy. "Git?"

"It seemed appropriate," Lucy said. "I got a report from the crime scene."

"On the murder," David said. "That's why I am here."

"Before that," Abby said very quickly. "I am now a short a deputy. I want to promote Paige to Head Deputy, which would entitle her to a raise, and hire her cousin Shaun as her replacement."

"Wow, you said that really fast," the Mayor said in a tone that only a politician could make. Then he looked at Paige. Smiled in a completely different way. Then looked at Lucy. "You good with that, deputy?"

"Yes, Mayor," Lucy said with a curt nod.

"Actually, as you know, the city council and I met last night," David said. "I managed to persuade them to increase your budget. So raises for everyone. I'll work out the details with you later, Sheriff. I know your cousin. Nice guy. I think he will be a good fit. You do know you will be required to wear a uniform?"

"Sheriff and I already discussed that," Paige replied, smile never waning.

"Good. Good." He turned to Abby. "Well, now the drama is over. Let's talk murder."

CHAPTER 11

The Mayor was settled down behind one of the desks. Abby was sitting on top of it. Lucy leaned against one another with a small notepad in one hand. They all took a sip of their coffee and savored it. Abby looked up and nodded.

"We all know the victim was Jimmy Evans," Lucy said without looking at her notes. "He was coming back to town on a stolen Harley motorcycle. Interesting point, the guy who reported it stolen didn't own it. It was on loan from another guy, an army vet who ran a body shop in Las Vegas until two months ago. Bottom line, Walt notified the guy. Apparently, he was a little more than annoyed. Back to Jimmy. We have no idea why he was coming back to town. They did find a notebook with five names written on the first page. He was shot..."

"Lucy," Abby said, holding up her hand. "The names, are they people in town?"

"Oh, I thought you'd find it more interesting he was shot four times with a .22," Lucy said. "Walt and I agree; whoever wanted Jimmy dead wanted to make sure. You never can be sure with such a small caliber round. Four bullets bouncing around inside Jimmy's skull would get the job done. His brain is probably mush."

"Well, thank you for that visual," Abby said.

"Which I really didn't need," Paige added.

"I could have lived without it," David agreed.

"Oh, sorry," Lucy said, not really looking sorry. "Walt and I were thinking, maybe the initial intention wasn't to kill Jimmy. Maybe they just wanted to scare him off."

"Going on that thought," Abby said. "Jimmy skidded to a stop. Our killer just decided to kill, or Jimmy said something to make the killer shoot him. Four times. Names, please, Lucy."

"Oh, Keanu Watershaw, Kirk James, Allison May Town, Lizzie Eastbourne, Lionel and...Merry Jo Anderson."

"Did you say Merry Jo?" Abby asked, looking a bit surprised.

"That is an odd mix," David said with a frown, ignoring Abby's question. "The town beauty queen, the town guy with issues, the town royal, and Lionel. Merry Jo? She lives in New York now."

"Not anymore," Lucy said, looking at Abby. "Josh Williams, out by her place, says he saw her move back over the weekend."

"She's here?" Abby asked.

"That's interesting," The Mayor said. "You will need to talk to them all. Those should all be interesting conversations. Don't forget to bow before talking to Lizzie."

"You really don't believe that about Lizzie?" Paige asked. "I like her. She is my best friend, but is she connected to one of England's oldest, richest families?"

"It was more her mother and grandmother," Abby said, but something distracted her. "They believed it. Said they had the evidence to prove it. Getting teased by the non-royal kids kind of burned Lizzie out on the idea. I heard she is leaving town."

"I heard that about you, too," Paige said with a smirk.

"Your promotion and raise aren't official yet," Abby snapped. Then took a sip of coffee. "Keanu? Kirk? Allison May? Talk about being at different ends of the spectrum."

"Keanu and James are about his age," David said. "Allison May is closer to your age. That makes her older than Jimmy. Then there is Lionel. What is that all about? I don't get Merry Jo. I know she hated him."

"Yes, she did, with good reason," Abby mumbled. Then more to herself, "Why the hell is she back?"

"You could ask her," Lucy said in a hesitant voice.

"Good news, it gives me somewhere to start," Abby said, ignoring Lucy while looking into her empty cup. She stood, approached the coffee pot, filled her cup, and turned around. "I'll start interviewing my suspects tomorrow. Paige, you will be with me. Lucy, you will be on regular duty, but keep yourself open to being called out for backup. All jokes aside, we have a dead body here. We have a murderer."

"So, you are training me?" Paige asked, confused. Do I really need training?"

"Yes. Lucy went to the academy. I got sent to those training courses in Cornwall. Plus, Phil and Bruce worked under my dad. Call Shaun, see if he can start tomorrow." She turned to the Mayor. So, how much grief are you and the city council going to give me?"

"None. It's not your fault Jimmy got himself killed outside of town. It looks like you have things well in hand." David stood and stretched. "Between you and me, I don't think the murderer is local. I think trouble followed Jimmy back home. But you are the Sheriff. You know better than me."

"Yeah, I'm the expert all of a sudden," Abby said, sipping her coffee. "I will be working with the state. Hopefully, they come up with something we can use. Odd choice for a weapon. I mean, pretty sure everyone in town has a rifle or shotgun. A whole lot less have pistols. A .22. What do you use that for?"

"Target practice," David said with a nod. "If you believe T.V. and the movies, it is the preferred caliber of hitmen."

"Four shots. Not a pro," Abby said. "Thanks for coming by, Mayor."

"Anytime, Abby." He turned and smiled at Paige. "Paige. Deputy."

All three women watched him walk out. Abby and Lucy looked at Paige. She looked back. "What?"

"You don't have anything going on with the mayor?" Lucy asked.

"Not yet," Abby said. "Small town, we would have heard about it. No, the Mayor is just sniffing around my new head deputy."

"Sniffing. That's gross!" Paige said, trying to look offended.

"I will be in my office," Abby said, heading toward it. I will be investigating the clues until lunch. I will make important calls only. I didn't get breakfast. I am running off coffee. You have been warned."

That said, the Sheriff went into her office and shut the door. Feet back in the bottom drawer, leaning back, eyes closed. Abby really did ponder the clues. She loved a good mystery, but Jimmy's murder was not on her mind.

A loud crack of thunder made her look up. Then the rain started. Abby muttered a curse, got up, and walked out. She headed for the front door. "I'll be out for a while."

Paige almost asked where she was going, but Lucy shook her head.

CHAPTER 12

Abby sat in her car, watching the rain pound down the windshield. This was Oregon. It rained there. She didn't mind the rain. Hell, she had lived in New York, a town with some of the country's coldest, most miserable winters. Pipes freezing, roads blocked by snow. Sometimes, it got so bad that many considered offering a sacrifice to the gods.

A virgin...if they could find one.

Abby liked to walk in the rain. Sometimes. Usually, when she was in a blue mood. At times like this, she believed the world was as gloomy as she was. Though more angry than sad, she was in one of those moods as she drove. She pulled the hood on her raincoat and climbed out of the car.

Merry Jo's farm wasn't a working farm. At least she didn't work it. She leased the land out to locals. Not that she needed the money. There was a small house and barn. Like most houses in Digger's Cove, the house looked like it had been built in the forties. It was called a Craftsman design with a front covered porch. Whatever the hell that meant. The house looked like it had been fixed up. The last time she had been there, it looked pretty run down. She looked toward the barn. It, too, looked well-kept, with a new roof and what looked like new windows. Abby said to herself, "Are you staying?"

There were no lights on in the house. A flickering light came out the open doors of the barn. Abby lowered her head to escape the downpour with her hands shoved into her raincoat pockets. She approached the doors and watched a tall woman with long, raven hair twisted into a single braid that reached her waist. A welding mask covered the face of the woman, who was using a torch on what looked like a mess of pipes and bars to Abby. She took in the tight, ripped jeans but not as a fashion statement and whitish tan top. The sheriff's stomach flipped. Even with a mask, the woman was beautiful.

Abby banged the door with her fist. The dark-haired woman looked up. She stared at Abby for a moment before turning off the torch. She lifted the mask, revealing a beautiful face with green eyes and lips that most women would kill for. Dark freckles dotted her nose and cheeks. A small smile came to those lips but then vanished.

"I thought we had an agreement?" Abby said in a cold tone.

"No, you thought we had an agreement," Merry Jo said, taking off the mask and tossing it down. She began to undo the braid. "I never agreed to anything."

"Why are you here?" Abby snapped.

"It's my hometown," she said, shaking her hair. It fell down in thick waves around her beautiful face. Merry Jo tossed back her hair and pushed it behind her ear. The woman seemed to radiate sexual energy. "This is where I was born and raised."

"You may have been raised here but don't belong here. I don't know why you came back, and I don't care. Go back to New York."

"Is that why you came out here, Sheriff?" Merry Jo said, tossing back her hair again and grinning. The smile reminded Abby of a cat playing with a mouse. "Tell me to leave town?"

"You probably heard Jimmy Evans was murdered outside of town," Abby said, moving closer.

"I heard about Jimmy. You look good. So we can't go back to the way it was?

"I was different back then. Younger."

"Now you are older and wiser?"

"Merry Jo, I just came out here because of the murder."

"I didn't know Jimmy that well. Do you think I killed him? You think I could do that?"

"Of all my suspects, you are the one I think is most capable of killing someone. I just don't see why you would."

"Thank you, I think," Merry Jo said, moving closer. "Everyone in this town thinks I am bitch. They might be right. I now see that. Still, I was hurt. You really thought I could do that?"

"Yes, we grew up together. Friends for life."
"

That changed in New York. I was alone...confused."

"Confused for two years?" Abby said, rolling her eyes. We were happy. Then your dad came to visit. You changed. You told him we weren't a couple but still wanted his approval."

"It was a mistake," Abby muttered.

"After you left. You changed. You focused on your job. I heard you became just another Wall Street shark. You got engaged to that jerk because being married looked good on the resume. Why did you keep putting off the wedding date?"

"I was busy with work." Abby snapped.

"Is that what you tell yourself, Abby? You can lie to yourself all you want. I know why you have yet to return to New York. It was because I was there."

"It takes money to move and live in New York," Abby snapped, her face blushing.

"Is that what you tell everyone? Tell yourself? You went to New York with nothing, built a career, and were supposed to get married. The American dream. The guy did turn out to be a jerk. So you were saved from a messy divorce. You came home and stayed."

"My father got sick, and you took advantage of that," Abby growled.

"That's a lie, and you know it. There was wine, but it wasn't the wine. You came to me. You didn't go to your fiancé. I know you broke off the engagement, not him. I happen to know you are sitting on three hundred thousand dollars. Daddy's life insurance covered the funeral and gave you a nice nest egg. You forget you told me about that."

"Bitch, I am not gay."

"It's not about being gay or straight. It's about love and being honest with yourself. Your daddy is not around to judge you anymore."

"You're staying?" Abby asked with a cold stare.

"One of us had to make a move. I am not going anywhere, Abby. You have the money to go back to New York. Go back. I'll stay here. I do my best work here."

Abby ignored the remark and asked, "Jimmy had your name in a notebook. You know why?"

"No idea. Jimmy didn't like me," Merry Jo said. "He thought of himself as a lady's man. He was offended that I didn't jump into the sack with him.

Abby, let's not fight."

"There is nothing to argue about. That's old history," Abby snapped. "Half the male population in Digger's Cove chased you."

"The key word in your statement is male. You are the one who caught me. I have known what I am since high school and have accepted it. Embraced it. And guess what? Digger's Cove doesn't care. Ask me. Ask Shaun."

"I may move back to New York. Abby said.

"You can move anywhere you want, Abby. But I am staying here. Funny, I hear a lot of people in town already suspected you were gay. You still got elected,"

"They didn't believe the rumors."

"When was the last time you had a date with a man...or woman?" Merry Jo asked, moving so close their faces were almost touching. The two women just stared at each other for the longest time.

"There has never been anyone since you," Merry Jo said softly. "Lovers, but you were always in my head and heart."

"Well, you're here," Abby broke the standoff, looking down and muttered. "Don't leave town until I say so."

"I am not going anywhere," Merry said, reaching up and pushing the hood off Abby's face. "Sorry, just wanted a better look."

They were still another long, quiet moment. Abby reached up, pushing the long hair away from Merry Jo's face. "Why did you come back?"

"I had to. When you think about it...you will understand."

Abby quickly turned and stormed out of the barn. She got to her car and banged on the hood several times before getting in. Then Abby banged the dashboard. She turned on the windshield wipers and looked up at the barn. Merry Jo stood at the door. She waved and went back into the barn. Abby closed her eyes and leaned back in the seat. Then sat up and started the car.

CHAPTER 13

Abby sat back in her chair, looking at nothing. Her head was spun with images, trying to ignore the occasional thoughts of Merry Jo that kept popping into her head.

Always smiling. Always looking so confident.

She muttered to herself and pulled open a drawer. She stared down into it for a moment before taking out an old Polaroid. It was a picture of her and Merry Jo. Younger. Happier. She tossed it back in and slammed the drawer closed. "Crap!"

She opened the file on Jimmy's murder and started to read. Abby really didn't consider herself a cop. Definitely not a detective. But this was interesting. Jimmy really was risking his life coming back to town. She had no doubt when push came to shove, especially to protect his grandson, his father would shoot him. But likely, James would then walk into her office and tell her he had just shot his son.

Or would he?

Would the insurance be canceled if he killed his son? The money wasn't going to him, but from what she knew about insurance companies, they would use any excuse not to pay.

Especially a million bucks.

So maybe James wouldn't walk in and confess.

She just couldn't see Lisa doing it. Lisa had her son to think about.

The five names Jimmy had in his pocket.

Keanu Watershaw was odd, but he was also a certified genius. Graduated high school at thirteen. Went off to MIT. Got three degrees in three years. Stayed at MIT for years but then had some kind of breakdown. Came home. Stayed up on his property doing his own private research. According to a friend she had at Oregon State Tech, he still published papers that were considered brilliant.

Then she thought about Jimmy. Did Keanu have money? Abby needed to find out if this was all about money.

Kirk James had money.

Well, his family did.

Probably more than millions. Billions. If you believe the town gossip. How Kirk had redesigned the family home that took some serious cash. But Kirk was harmless. More importantly, Kirk never left his house. At least, not that she knew of. It wasn't like Abby had any reason to watch his house. She would have to go talk to him.

Allison May Towns? She was the embodiment of a beauty queen, not just by looks and body but the whole bubbly personality thing. She had been in the running for Miss Oregon. From there, it was a hop, skip, and jump to Miss America. It didn't happen. She got into the top ten. Now twenty-nine years old. Was she too old for the beauty queen thing? What was she doing these days? Allison May had money. Some kind of trust fund.

How much?

On the other hand, would the town head cheerleader, homecoming queen, prom queen, and Valedictorian give a loser like Jimmy the time of day? Sitting in the middle of the street in one of her short, tight dresses with a gun, Allison May would make Jimmy stop. It would also make a good movie poster. That just made Abby laugh. Then she remembered that Allison May was much smarter than people gave her credit.

Then there was Lizzie Eastbourne. If you believed her mom and grandmother, they were related to British Royalty. The kids in school had given her a hard time, calling her princess and Your Highness. She had graduated and attended a two-year state college but needed more money to attend a four-year university. Smart. Really smart. But college is expensive. Now, she was a cocktail waitress at the only bar in town. Bitter. Maybe. But why would she kill Jimmy?

That left Lionel.

Every town had one. A guy who just walked his own path. Graduated high school. Had the brains to get more than passing grades in high school but showed no interest in furthering his education. Nice enough guy. Worked the pump and did some oil changes at the service stations, along with other odd jobs. Lionel seemed to have no real ambition. He just drifted through life. There had been a couple of complaints. Lionel was peeking into windows. She talked about that to Lionel and thought it had been worked out. She had a chat with Lionel. I'm not saying he was a peeping Tom, but if it turns out, he is. He could end up in prison, and someone like him wouldn't do well in prison.

That worked because there had been no more complaints - or Lionel got smarter.

But Lionel had been friends with Jimmy. Lionel was one of the few, the only person in town who actually liked Jimmy.

Abby whirled around and looked at the corkboard mounted on the wall. It was covered with flyers and wanted posters. Most of it had been up there when her father was in office. Most of the wanted posters were yellow. The sheriff got up, took them down, and tossed the papers into the trash. She found some index cards in her bottom drawer, along with some Sharpies. Red, green, and black. She wrote Jimmy Evans' name on a black ink card. Under it, in red ink, she wrote the following questions: Why was he coming back, who knew, and why was he dead? She pinned that card on the top corner of the board. Another card she wrote in green, Skidded to stop. Shot four times in the face. This was pinned by the first card. Then she wrote the names James Evans, Lisa Evans, Keanu Watershaw, Kirk James, Allison May Towns, Lizzy Eastbourne, and Lionel. Each name is written on a separate card in black with a big, red question mark beside each one. Once all the cards were on the board, she leaned back and said, "Well, it is a start. More coffee."

Abby exited her office and beelined for the coffee machine. Paige was standing by her desk holding up a tan uniform, still on the hanger, studying it with a critical eye. Standing beside her was a short, slim man with short black hair. He had a nice-looking round face, with kind eyes and, well, a weak jaw. His bright red shirt and black pants fit him perfectly. Abby poured some coffee and smiled. "Shaun, I assume being here means you are interested in the job."

"Oh, hi, Sheriff," he said with a big smile. He approached Abby to shake her hand. "Considering it. The uniform only comes in tan? I like the dark blue uniforms they wear in Los Angeles."

"Sorry, only tan," Abby said with a smile. "It's kind of a tradition. But you are going to be in the station most of the time. You could just go casual."

"Oh no, Sheriff, I want to be part of the team. Paige said I don't have to wear a gun. Not a fan."

"No, it is mostly paperwork, answering the phone, and handling the radio. Just keep things moving along."

"I can do that." He returned to the uniform, took it from Paige, and held it up. "Am I allowed to alter it?"

"Knock yourself out. So that completes the interview. Am I hiring you?"

"Oh yes, yes," Shaun said, returning and shaking Abby's hand again. "Thank you, and I won't let you down."

"In Digger's Cove? Little chance of that." She said, sipping from her cup. Her stomach growled loud enough for Paige and Shaun to look at her. "No breakfast. Not even a donut. We should look into getting donuts to have with our morning coffee."

"My hips don't need donuts," Paige said.

"You don't have to eat them," Abby said with a smile. "I am going to look into getting donuts."

"Before or after the murder investigation?" Paige asked.

"I can do both at the same time. I worked for a major corporation. I learned to multi-task from the best. Paige, get the paperwork done for Shaun. Issue him as many uniforms as he wants and any other equipment he might need. I am taking an early lunch."

"Consider it done," Paige said. "Anything else?"

"Yes, find me a poster board, magic markers...and more push pins."

"Election is not until next year, and you don't need any posters. No one is going to run against you."

"I need them for the investigation. Jimmy? Dead? Shot? Need to get my thoughts straight in my head. You should start thinking, too. You will be my...my..."

"Watson to your Holmes?" Shaun said.

"Hasting to your Poirot?" Paige said.

"Hastings? Hastings wasn't that bright," Shaun said. "More like Natalie to Monk."

"Monk?" Paige asked, sounding surprised. "Wasn't Monk a brilliant detective?"

"Yes, but he had issues," Shaun said.

"I am going to lunch and pretending you two just didn't insult your boss," Abby said, moving toward the door. "I still want the poster board and markers."

CHAPTER 14

Abby walked out of the station and headed across the street. She nodded to the mayor, who was across the street. He nodded back. Lionel rushed up beside her. He was in his thirties, but his body language suggested some immaturity. Brown hair cut in a manner that screamed fifties. Slicked back with Brylcreem. The black-and-white sneakers, jeans, white tee-shirt, and letterman's jacket continued this look. The leather jacket was red and purple.

"Hi, Sheriff. Is it true?" Lionel asked, trying to keep pace with Abby, who seemed more interested in getting across the street to the diner than talking—at least at the moment.

"Is what true?" Abby knew what he was asking about but couldn't think of anything else to say.

"Jimmy Evans got shot right outside of town." Lionel looked more excited than he should. "Geez, who would have thought. Jimmy, just shot down like that."

"Like what?" Abby stopped and looked right in the man's face. He looked down at his sneakers. "How did you know he was shot? I know there were few secrets in Digger's Cove, but I don't think anyone should know he was shot...so quickly."

"Oh, oh, I see, I see," Lionel said, looking up very nervously. "Pretty good, Sheriff. Catching me off guard like that. Well, you know Bobby Dryer, he makes deliveries to Cornwall. He was coming back and saw all the police cars. A state police officer waved him through. Bobby asked what had happened. The police officer said someone had been shot. By the time he got back to town, Ethel Thomas, who owns the farm right by that road, already knew it was Jimmy Evans. It didn't take long for word to spread through town. I just wanted to make sure it was true. Could all be gossip?"

"It's not gossip," Abby said, putting her hands on her hips and smiling. "You were pretty good friends with Jimmy. You seem to be taking it pretty well."

"That was back in high school. We hung out. I didn't like some of the stuff Jimmy did...I wasn't into chasing girls."

"I can see that, but you do like to look at girls. Have you been behaving?"

"I don't do that anymore, Sheriff. You made it clear next time, I would get arrested. I really don't want to go to jail. I really don't. You believe that, Sheriff?"

"Lionel, no one wants to go to prison. Not even the guys who deserve to go. Don't want to go to prison? No more windows."

Lionel's head popped back up. "No, Sheriff. No more windows. Is it a crime to see someone do something bad and not tell you?"

"It depends on what bad thing they did."

"What he did to Lisa was wrong," Lionel said, looking down at his sneakers. "Jimmy leaving town was the best thing for Lisa and their son. Mr. Evans would have shot him if he hadn't left town. At least, that's what Jimmy told me before he skipped."

"That's funny," Abby said, stepping closer. "What you just did there. Smart, very smart. I didn't think you had that in you. Changing the subject. You asked me a question. Then, suddenly, we talk about Jimmy again. Pretty funny."

"I guess that's right," Lionel said and nervously laughed.

"So you didn't know he was coming back to town?" Abby asked, smiling but looking right into his face. "Because that would be important for me to know. Better for you if you tell me. Now."

"No, no. How would I know that?" He stepped back, but Abby moved with Lionel until he bumped into a parked car.

"Here's the problem," Abby said, moving even closer. "Jimmy had a notebook with your name on it. Why would he have that? Sounds like you might be lying to me. You got something to tell me?"

The mayor was kneeling beside a beautiful 1955 Corvette, studying the car. Lionel looked terrified. He began to sputter and wipe away nonexistent sweat from his face.

"Abby, sorry to interrupt," David said, standing up and looking over with a smile. "I have to leave my car overnight. You're not going to ticket me."

Abby, annoyed, looked over and gave a you've got to be kidding me look. "Mayor, a little busy here. You know we don't ticket you."

"My bad. Lionel, you listen to the Sheriff." With that, he walked off.

"Now, where were we?" Abby growled, trying to get back in control of the conversation.

"Sheriff, I didn't know he was coming back. Really," Lionel said, now looking terrified. "I didn't know and didn't see anything. Honest to God."

"Okay. For now. We will be talking again. Lionel, I can tell you are holding something back. I will find out what it is," Abby said, stepping back but not smiling. She tugged at his jacket. "New jacket? You're a fighting otter now?"

"I got it cheap at Liddy's," he said, straightening his jacket. The old one was getting pretty beat up. I am still looking for a good leather one."

"Vintage leather jackets can be hard to find," Abby said, "and expensive." She turned away, stepping onto the curb. She paused, looking back at him. "Remember, we will be talking soon. Don't be leaving town."

"Me? I'll never leave Digger's Cove. I love this town."

"Yeah," Abby said. "You still renting a room at Becki's house?"

"No, I moved. Small place up by the Donner Farm."

"I knew that. Just seeing if you would lie about it."

"I am not lying." Lionel sniffed and walked away. "You have no right to do this to me."

Abby watched him walk off and said, "Sure, as there is a God, you know something. And I will know what it is."

CHAPTER 15

"Steak and eggs, over easy, hash browns, and white bread, toasted?" Suzie asked. The nineteen-year-old waitress had followed Abby to a back booth. Her pink uniform and white apron were clean, except for a red stain on the apron. She was a cute redhead with short hair and a full figure.

"Yes, thanks, Suzie," Abby said, sitting down and looking up. "Coffee and orange juice."

"The usual. I am surprised," the waitress said. "Considering you were looking at a dead body and all this morning."

"I have seen dead bodies," Abby said, turning over the coffee cup on the table and nodding toward it. "Lived in New York."

"Not here."

"People die here. Old man Jenkins, just last week. He was working in his basement and just fell over. Dead. Then there was Louise Davis last month."

"Heart attack and stroke," Suzie said, grabbing a coffee pot from the waitress station. "Not murdered. Shot."

"Ray Wallins shot Dennis Leery," Abby said, smiling as her coffee cup was filled.

"That was a hunting accident, and Dennis lived. Granted, he still has a limp and doesn't hunt anymore, but this was murder. You were looking at a murdered body and are in here, eating like it was no big deal."

"It is a big deal. The state police have said it's my problem." She poured sugar into her coffee.

"Really? You? They expect you to solve a murder?"

"Yes. Me." Abby looked annoyed. "I am the sheriff. It's kind of my job."

"Any suspects?" Suzy asked with a shrug.

"Yes, you right now."

"Excuse me, way too old for me, but even as a kid, I didn't like Jimmy Evans?" Suzy put her hands on her hips, staring at Abby. "Your list would be shorter if you just listed the people who liked him."

"Who did like him? Lionel denies they were friends."

"Huh, that is a good question." The waitress looked up at the ceiling, then looked down with a smile. "Before he got Lisa pregnant, my mom said he was sniffing around Merry Jo."

"Merry Jo? Are you sure? She wouldn't give him the time of day."

"My mom said he was sniffing. She didn't say he was getting anywhere. Now we all know he was wasting his time."

"Yes, now we all know," Abby huffed. "I suppose you heard she is back in town."

"Yeah, that's right. Back out on the family farm, all alone, making all those sculptures. Looks like junk to me."

"You know how much they pay for that junk in New York, Boston, and Los Angeles?"

"So that's true," Suzy conceded. "She makes serious money from that stuff. Why did she come back here?"

"You are asking the wrong person. You going to put in my order?"

"Right away, Abby." She took the catsup bottle off the table. "I better get your fresh bottle. This one is only half full. I assume you are going to bury that perfectly cooked steak in catsup."

"I like catsup."

"You must because you can't even taste the steak under how much you put on."

"You are affecting your tip."

"Your last tip was nothing to brag about," Suzie said, walking off before Abby could respond.

Abby pulled out her notebook and wrote something inside. "Merry Jo. Jimmy was stupid. As if he had a chance with Merry Jo. Gay or not."

CHAPTER 16

Abby leaned back in her chair, staring at the index cards pinned to the corkboard. Beside it was a poster board with a crudely drawn picture of the crime scene. It was basically two straight lines with stick figures. One was lying on the ground. The other was standing over it with a badly-drawn pistol. An even worse drawing of a motorcycle was by the dead body. "Why did you stop, Jimmy? Why did you stop? Were you meeting someone? Or was it a complete surprise?"

"I can draw a better picture if you want," Paige said, stepping into the office.

"It serves its purpose. I don't need a Rembrandt to ponder." Abby looked over. "Must be quitting time."

"Must be," Paige said. "You staying late?"

"Got a murder," Abby said with a shrug. "You know what the key is. The key is, why was Jimmy coming home? I figure that out, and I know my murderer."

"I have been thinking about that," Paige said. "It's got to be money. A lot of money. I know we joke about it, and Mr. Evans might not have killed Jimmy, but he would made sure he left town one way or another. He wouldn't want Jimmy close to his grandson."

"He used the shotgun to make Jimmy sign some papers before he let him leave town. A sound beating would make Jimmy get on his stolen bike and leave. I didn't know Jimmy well, but I did know he was like most bullies: a coward at heart." Abby rubbed her eyebrows while sighing. "We'll start with Kirk James and move on to Allison May. Keanu is over in Cornwall for a day or two. According to Suzie, down at the diner, Jimmy was sniffing around Merry before he left town."

"Sniffing?"

"Her word, not mine. We both know Jimmy was wasting his time, but we should talk to her."

"And you haven't?" Page asked.

Once again annoyed, Abby looked up at Paige and then sighed. "Yes, but..."

"But what? I don't see the motive for Merry Jo."

"Neither do I. But if any could kill someone, it would be Merry Jo."

"Really?" Paige leaned against the wall, smiling. "Is that Sheriff Abby talking or Abby, my friend? People have noticed you haven't dated for a while."

"I intimidate the local men." Abby stood up and stretched. "Probably the badge and uniform."

"Maybe, but it might be the vibe you put out."

"I don't put out a vibe."

"Yes, you do. It's kind of a don't mess with me vibe. Of course, it would help if you did something with your hair. A little makeup, some lipstick..."

"Well, until I meet someone, I will just forgo the lipstick." Abby walked out the door. Paige followed her. "You will let me know if you start dating the mayor."

"I am not dating the mayor," Page said, sounding huffy.

"Not yet. I saw the way David was looking at you," Abby said without looking back. She went over to the radio and picked up the mic. "Phil, this is Abby. Over.

"Phil here, Sheriff," a voice crackled. "Over."

"Yeah, we're out of here. You're on your own until Bruce comes on." Abby waited a moment, then continued, "We had a murder, so stay on your toes. Call me at home if you need me. Over."

"Roger that, Sheriff. Over and out."

Abby put down the mic and walked around the office with Paige on her heels, turning off the lights. They ended up by the front door. Abby looked at Paige. "No uniforms?"

"Oh, Shaun took them home," Paige said. "We're going to alter them and iron them. Want to look sharp on my first day as a Head Deputy."

"Paige, we joke about Digger's Cove, but we got a murderer out there. You will be out on the streets. Be careful."

"You going to start carrying your gun?"

"Not yet."

CHAPTER 17

"You look all so...shiny and new," Abby said, staring at Paige and Shaun. They both wore the tan sheriff's uniforms, but unlike her own shirt, they fit perfectly and had been ironed and starched pants and shirts. Their badges and belts gleamed. Even the tan seemed brighter than Abby's. She noted Paige was wearing a pistol. Shaun was not. "I feel like I should go home, shower, and put on a fresh uniform,"

"There's no need for that, Sheriff," Shaun said. You definitely don't need a shower. I could iron a shirt for you right now."

"We don't have an iron here."

"We do now," Shaun said. I set an ironing board up in the back with the other uniforms." He smiled. We only have time to get one uniform done."

"Thanks, I am good," Abby said, turning and spotting a white box on the coffee table. She walked over and peeked in. "Oh, donuts! I am a happy camper."

"You did mention donuts yesterday," Paige said, coming over. "Shaun brought them in."

"I didn't know what kind you liked, so I got a variety," Shaun said, stepping forward.

"I like all donuts." Abby took out a Boston Crème. Paige poured her a cup of coffee and held it out. The sheriff took the coffee and smiled. "Let me enjoy my breakfast, and we will be out of here."

Abby headed toward her office, stopped, and turned around. She watched them pour coffee. "You guys aren't going to eat the donuts, are you?"

They just stood there looking amused.

"Fine, more for me."

An hour later, Abby and Paige were walking up a driveway behind tall trees.

"You have been here since the remodeling?" Abby asked.

"No, but I heard. I am really curious."

Abby just nodded as they continued up the driveway and around the trees. A two-story house, white with red trim, sat on a series of poles holding the entire house a good ten feet above the ground. A metal tube came down from the bottom of the house to the ground. A door was built into the tube. They walked up to the tube.

"Aside from the poles holding the entire house off the ground and the tube, it looks normal," Paige said.

"Hmm, wait until you get inside," Abby said, pressing a red button on the side of the tube.

"Starship Ventura, identity yourselves," a voice asked from a speaker mounted somewhere.

"Sheriff Abby Anderson and Deputy Walton. Permission to come aboard, captain."

"Ah, the local law enforcement. I hear of an incident in this sector. Permission to come aboard granted."

The door slid open. Abby and Paige stepped in. The door closed. A hum filled the tube as the elevator rose up into the house. The door opened a second later. They entered a room with purple walls and a single console set up by a door. A woman in her late twenties stood by the console. She was dressed in a short, tight, blue dress uniform like women wore on the series' first run. Her brown hair was pinned up into an old beehive style. She walked up to Abby and smiled. "Good to see you, Abby."

"You too, Nancy," Abby said with a nod. "How is he today?"

"Better than expected. Since you are here, you must know that Kirk knew the man who was killed. He has been working on a report for you."

"So we are expected," Abby said. I assume the family gave you another raise since you are still here."

"I got my bachelor's and master's," Nancy said. I thought I could pursue my PHD since they are paying for it. They agree I can write a book, but they get a first look."

"Six years here with Kirk," Abby said. "You are a better woman than me."

"Oh, it's not that bad. Kirk doesn't try to get me into bed because I am the ship's doctor," Nancy said. "I assume you know he has occasional female visitors."

"Many in costume. I, along with the rest of the town, have noticed. Some beautiful women in very skimpy outfits. I don't need to know who or what they are."

"The ladies are part of the therapy. It gives him some social interaction. Adds to the fantasy and keeps him calm. I think I should tell you something. Is it true the victim was coming from Las Vegas?"

"Yes, why?"

"He was in Vegas a couple months ago for a convention. It went so well. He was able to interact with so many people. It gave him a lot of freedom. I lost track of him a couple of times. Once for over an hour."

"Thanks, Nancy," Abby said. "Shall we go to the bridge?"

CHAPTER 18

The three women walked to an elevator building the wall. The red door opened. They stepped in. After the door closed, it was a short ride to the second floor. They stepped out into a small-scale exact replica of the bridge on the Starship Enterprise. The command chair sat in the middle of the room. Two women dressed in red mini-dresses sat at a control board right in the chair. Both were young and attractive, hair pinned into fancy 1960s styles.

Kirk James sat in the command chair wearing a gold commander's shirt. He was a chubby, clean-shaven man with short blond hair. He looked a little like a young Captain Kirk.

Abby stopped Nancy and whispered, "Are those?"

"Yes, therapists. Paid by the hour, so don't feel you have to rush," Nancy said with a smile.

"Two?" Paige asked as she took it all in.

"His stamina has improved over the last year. The captain did have a reputation," she said. "The family is quite pleased."

"How many cameras did the city council let you put up?" Abby asked.

"Twenty. All in public places. We also have a lot of space footage. This helps in the illusion. He actually..."

"Ah, Sheriff Anderson!" Kirk said, noticing the newcomers. He jumped up from the chair and rushed over. "It's been too long. But I understand. We both have our duties. Is this the new deputy? I don't believe we've met."

"This Head Deputy Paige Walton," Abby said. "Just promoted. You look well."

"I'm Pleased to meet you, Head Deputy Walton," Kirk said, shaking Paige's hand but then holding onto it. A smile came to his lips as he looked over the beautiful woman. You must allow me to give you a tour of the ship."

"Captain, they are here on official business," Nancy said with a smile. "The incident on the road."

"Oh yes, sadly, we were not scanning that area at the time," the man said with a shake of his head. He returned to his command chair and picked up a small, square, plastic computer disk. "I made a full report. I can tell you this: I attended the academy with James Evans. Not a very good cadet. Low grades and very undisciplined. Got into some trouble. Concerning a young lady, I believe. She was a cadet, too, but had to drop out. A loss for Starfleet."

"I don't suppose you've seen Mr. Evans here?" Abby asked, taking the disk.

"In this sector? Oh no, it was my understanding that he was banned. Local trouble, which you probably know all about."

"Yes, yes, how about another sector?" Abby asked.

"I was just about to bring that up." Kirk smiled. "I attended a Starfleet Conference. Nothing significant, just connecting with other commanders and such. I had a wonderful time. Made several new friends. Promised to visit my ship. But I am getting off track. I was having lunch with a charming ensign when Mr. Evans walked up to my table. There is no introduction, but he grabs my hand and starts acting like we are old friends. He was upsetting my lunch companion, so I excused myself. Got right to the point. No surprise. He asked me for money. I pointed out to him money was no longer used. He became quite indignant. Lost control of himself. Started to insult me and my rank. Thankfully, the local security came to my rescue. I was able to return to my charming ensign."

"Did he make any threats?" Abby asked.

"Some nonsense about going to my family, which is absurd. The only relative I have is a nephew. I have no idea where he is. Ran off. I must say, it was quite upsetting."

"So you went back to lunch with your friend, and that was the last you saw of him?" Paige asked.

"It was my last conversation with him," Kirk said. "He started to follow the ensign and me to my suite. Thankfully, security stepped in again. I saw him skulking around the convention, but he kept his distance. That reminds me, I promised to call the ensign."

"Captain," Nancy said with a severe tone. "If you recall. The Ensign is coming for a visit next week."

"Oh, that's right," Kirk said with a laugh. "The downside to commanding a starship. You get busy and forget things."

"Captain, do you ever scan the road leading into town?" Abby asked.

"Of course, the only road into your small town. Oh, I see what you're asking. Do I have any footage from the day of the crime? We should. I will check, and if I find anything, I will send it to you immediately."

"I would be happy to deliver it," Nancy said.

"Excellent, Doctor," he said, looking a little distracted.

Abby noticed Kirk look over at the two ladies at the control. They both smiled at him. She shook her head. "Well, Captain, I won't take up any more of your time. I am sure the doctor can show us to the teleport room."

"Thank you, Sheriff." Kirk started to walk away but stopped and looked back. "Oh, Sheriff, could you speak to that young man who keeps trespassing on this property? I know this is your town, but this is Federation property."

"What, young man?" Abby asked.

"Lionel. I don't know him well, but he seems too interested in Federation business."

"I'll speak to him. Today. I promise. Don't forget to check for those records."

CHAPTER 19

"I don't like the idea of Lionel wandering around the property," Nancy said, standing by the red tube. "He seems nice enough, but putting it delicately? I wouldn't mind getting him on the couch."

"I would be interested in what you find out," Paige said. "Is that ensign really coming here?"

"Oh yes, I am very excited," Nancy said with a smile. "This will be his first outside visitor. She is as much into the Star Trek world as Kirk but is not trapped in it. I have spoken with her and her family. The Ensign doesn't see what the problem is. The family is quite happy that she has made such a good friend. It helps that Kirk's family is rich."

"Okay, I now know Jimmy tried to hit up Kirk for money," Abby said. Luckily, he didn't get any but kept hanging around. Nancy, how much damage could Jimmy have done to Kirk if he had gotten inside the house and tried to convince him this was all a lie?"

"Before we started all this," Nancy said, "Kirk just sat in his room and watched Star Trek. The original series, over and over. He started to believe he was part of that universe. The doctors I work with came up with this radical therapy. The family was willing to give it a try. It may seem strange, but it is working. Kirk is now interacting with people. His family comes here. They meet at the café. They talk and laugh. This is just the first step. We got him out of the house and to Las Vegas. The ensign coming here is huge. Evans showing up at this critical moment could undo all our work."

"Nancy, I need you to contact the family," Abby said. "I need to know if Jimmy tried to shake them down."

"Abby, you know who they are. You just don't call them." Nancy paused. "Oh my God. Do you think he was coming here to mess with Kirk? Blackmail the family...not a smart thing to do."

"Why?" Paige asked.

"You don't become as rich and powerful as James without breaking a few rules," Abby said. They would not like being blackmailed."

"Maybe they sent someone to stop Jimmy," Paige said.

"Maybe Jimmy stopped because he thought he was going to get some money," Abby said with a shrug. "Got a bullet in the head instead."

"More than one bullet," Paige said.

"I'll call the family," Nancy said.

CHAPTER 20

"Why, Abby, this is a delightful surprise," Allison May said with a smile that was too wide and white to be real. Her red hair was big, with curls reaching her very slender waist. The red top and white shorts were tight enough to show off her hourglass figure but in a tasteful manner. The blouse's neckline was high but hinted at a more than ample bosom. Despite the heavy makeup and lipstick, the lady was obviously quite beautiful with high cheekbones, button nose, and full lips that God had given to her. Allison looked twenty but was pushing thirty. She was born and raised in Digger's Cove, but after a beauty pageant in Alabama, she spoke with a Southern accent. "Please come in. You caught me at a bad time. Busy as a bee."

Abby and Paige followed Allison May into the front room. There were cardboard boxes stacked against the wall, and several open boxes were sitting around the nicely furnished room. The two officers took it in while their host fluttered around, picking up small items and putting them into one of the open boxes.

"Are we moving, Allison May?" Abby asked.

"Why yes, we are," Allison May said with another smile. "I am afraid it is time for this bird to fly. Digger's Cove had finally gotten too small for me."

"Trust fund kicked in?" Paige asked, looking really happy.

"Oh, Paige, you are just terrible," the blonde said, stopping, putting her hands on her hips, and giving Paige a hurt look. "Are you still upset about the whole prom queen thing?"

"No. Not that, or the head cheerleader thing, or class president thing. I was still annoyed about the whole thing with Bobby Huston. But I am over it. You look good."

"Thank you. Oh, Bobby was such a cutie, and those muscles..! Trust me, darling. He was good-looking and well-built but dumb as a post. I wonder where he ended up."

"Los Angeles. He runs a bar in West Hollywood that caters to the leather crowd. That's according to Shaun."

"Are you saying?" Allison said, putting her hand to her chest and looking shocked. Then she smiled. "But that explains so much. No more than a good night's kiss. I thought he was just being a gentleman. But he did look so good in that tuxedo at prom. So, what brings you here?"

"You haven't heard about Jimmy Evans?" Abby asked.

"Jimmy Evans?" She looked even more surprised. "What about Jimmy? The last time I saw him, he was in Las Vegas. I was a judge for a pageant. He completely embarrassed me. Flirting with me right in front of the other girls. He was still wearing that ridiculous letterman jacket. I suspected she hadn't bathed for a day or two between you and me. Disgusting. Look at me. As if."

"I will admit, you are out of his league," Abby said with a smile. "You knew him back in high school?"

"Oh, he was ahead of me." Allison May laughed. "He actually asked me out. As you know, I blossomed quite early in life. Poor Jimmy always had an exaggerated opinion of himself. Why are you asking about Jimmy?"

"Jimmy was coming back to town," Abby said. "Someone shot him before he got here. Out on the main road."

"Jimmy's dead? Murdered? Well, I think we can all agree that Jimmy getting murdered is not a big surprise. I am sure his daddy would have done it if he hadn't left town. Oh wait, you think I killed Jimmy? That is just so funny. Yes, I do have the skill. My granddaddy made sure I knew my way around a pistol or rifle. But I had no reason to kill Jimmy. He was nothing to me."

"I know this is rude to ask," Abby said, "but this is a murder investigation. Just how much did dear old granddaddy leave you in that trust?"

"That is a very personal question," Allison May said with a stiff smile and shake of her head that made her red curls bounce. "Mama and I had access to the trust for living expenses and paid for my pageant fees and all required to compete in them. Granddaddy was a big believer in my goals. When Mama passed away, a lot of money came to me, but the entire trust could only come to me in one of two ways. One was if I got married, my husband would have control of the money. Granddaddy was very old-fashioned. The second was that I graduated from college with an MBA or a law degree. Which I just achieved."

"What?" Paige asked, looking genuinely surprised. "You barely finished college. How did you get an MBA or a law degree?"

"But I did take a class on legal documents and how to read them," Allison said with a wicked smile. "Because of that class, how poorly written that clause in the trust was, and changes in the law, I got my degree from Sweetwater College of Law. Go, Raccoons!"

"Where the hell is Sweetwater College of Law?" Paige asked.

"I am more interested in how they came up with a raccoon for a mascot," Abby said. Let me guess: the school is online or down south—way down south."

"Online. It only took six months. But a law degree is a law degree. Granddaddy's lawyers objected until I passed the bar."

"You passed the bar?" Abby said. "I mean, I know you are smart."

"Oh, Abby, Sweetwater is a college that trains you to pass the bar. If I was to try to practice law, I would be in over my head. Since I have no intention of being a lawyer, I am fine."

"So you are moving where?" Abby asked.

"New York!" Allison May said with a smile.

"I hate you," Abby muttered. "So, Allison May, you have no idea why Jimmy had your name written in his little notebook."

"No idea. Did Jimmy come here to see me? Waste of time. I am on my way to a whole new life."

"No more pageants?" Paige asked.

"That is a young lady's game. I still have the looks and body to win, but we all get old. I am going to look into acting or producing. I certainly have the money for it."

"Well, good luck, Allison May," Abby said, turning to leave and then turning back. "So Jimmy couldn't have done anything to screw up your new life?"

"Not that I am aware of," the redhead said with another smile. "Honestly, I think my supposed lawyers are plotting against me. There used to be a third clause. If I had a male child, that's who would get the money. Once again, thanks to that class, I now know that it is illegal. Not that it was going to happen."

"Oh my god!" Paige said. "You really were the school tease. All those guys who bragged were lying? You lead them on?"

"Kissing, sometimes some heavy petting with my bra off, but no one got into these panties," Allison May said.

"Wait!" Paige gasped. "You're still..."

"A virgin? Yes. I couldn't take too many chances. We are talking a lot of money. Say I did get a bun in the oven. I would have been out all of the pageants, whether I kept the baby or not. My supposed lawyers would have kept me in court for years."

Abby asked, "You said he tried to seduce you in Vegas?"

"Oh my God, seduce? He suggested we get a drink and talk about old times. That's not seduction. Dinner with lobster and costly wine is seduction. Do you really think he was coming here for a second shot? Oh, that is rich. Talk about a wasted trip."

"When did you graduate from Raccoon U?" Abby asked.

"Three months ago," Allison said. "But, like I said, things are not completely settled. Now, if you will excuse me, the movers are coming tomorrow. But it was nice seeing you all."

CHAPTER 21

"Neither one has a motive," Paige said, leaning against the squad car. "Allison May could do it, but why would she? Kirk, I just don't see him leaving the house. He doesn't have a history of violence. Am I boring you?"

"I am listening," Abby said, stooping down and studying the grass in front of Allison May's house. She made a humming sound, got to her feet, and began to slowly walk across the lawn and around the house.

"Abby, where you going?" Paige followed her boss. She frowned and then asked, "Wait, are you using those tracking skills your father supposedly taught you? You weren't lying about that?"

"Why would I lie about something like that? I may not have ever shot a deer, but I sure the hell can track one," Abby said, slowly moving down the side of the house and stopping below a window. She looked around. A smile came to her face. The sheriff reached into the bushes and pulled out an old-fashioned metal milk crate. She put it down under the window and stood on it. "Not only a deer, but a person too."

"Oh my God, we have a peeping tom," Paige said, coming up by her boss. "Bedroom or bathroom?"

"Bedroom," Abby said, jumping down and smiling. When the window opened, she looked up, and Allison May stuck her head out. "Hi, Allison May."

"What the hell are you doing out there, Abby?" she asked, looking down and annoyed.

"It appears someone has been peeping in your window," Abby said. "You don't know who, do you?"

"Again?" She sighed. "You know who it is. It is the town weirdo. Lionel. You caught him before."

"Yeah, I guess the talk didn't work. Might be time to arrest Lionel." Abby sighed. "Good news, you are moving, so problem solved. On the other hand, this could be very useful."

"Not funny, Abby. The idea of him leering over my naked body is just creepy."

"Allison May, guys are leering over your body, naked or not," Paige said with a smirk.

"Really? Really, Paige. Maybe he is peeking through your window. I mean, you got a nice figure and all."

"Geez, I hadn't thought of that. I apologize." Paige turned to Abby. "Could you look around my house?"

"Right after I find the murderer," Abby said distractedly. "I'll have a car cruise by tonight. So don't go shooting my deputies."

"Why, Abby, are you trying to find out if I have a gun?" Allison May asked. "Aren't you being clever? I may know how to use a gun, but I don't own one. Sorry to disappoint you all. If I don't see you again, bye!"

The window closed. Abby shook her head and returned to the house's front carrying the milk crate. Once she reached the car, she closed the carton in the trunk.

"Hey, what did you mean Lionel starting to peep might be useful?"

"Lionel knows something. He hasn't told me yet, but tossing him in a cell may change that."

"What do you think he knows?

"I don't know." She smiled at Paige. "Do I want lunch, or should I go talk to Keanu? Lunch."

CHAPTER 22

"Let me guess: pastrami on a Kaiser roll with catsup. Cole slaw on the side, no pickle."

"You know what I like," Abby said, smiling at Irwin, who looked nothing like a deli owner. He was tall, thin, and had a bush of blond hair on top of his head. His nose and lips were too small for his broad face, while his eyes were too big. The black-framed glasses made them look even bigger.

"I refuse to put catsup on my wonderful pastrami," Irwin said with a sigh. "Pastrami requires mustard and pickles."

"I don't like mustard and pickles," Abby said. "Just give me the catsup, and I'll put it on myself."

"Why do you two always go through this?" Paige asked, leaning against the deli counter, looking bored while taking in the customers. Every time she comes here for lunch, the great catsup debate starts."

"I don't start it. Irwin does," Abby said. "He knows I don't like mustard and pickles."

"Who doesn't like mustard and pickles?" He asked.

"Me. When are you going to get a deep fryer in here so I can have fries with my sandwich?"

"A real deli doesn't have a deep fryer. You get your sandwich, then have coleslaw, potato salad, or macaroni salad. Maybe some potato chips."

"You don't carry potato chips."

"I am thinking about it," Irwin said. "There have been requests."

"I just requested French fries," Abby said with a smile.

"Okay, enough of this banter," Paige said, turning around. "I will have a turkey club with potato salad."

"Hey, Sheriff, is it true that Jimmy got his head blown off just outside of town?" Irwin asked.

"Not his head, but pretty much most of his face," Abby said, looking down into the display case. "Hey, that's new. Blue cheese potato salad."

"I saw it on TV last night and decided to try it out," Irwin said, picking up a tiny plastic spoon and taking a small sample of the potato salad. "Try it."

"I think I will," Abby said, taking the spoon.

"I am shocked. You're going to try something new."

"I try new stuff. It's just my options are limited in this town," Abby said and then tasted the salad. She chewed for a minute, nodded, and swallowed. "I will take that along with the coleslaw. It's too bad you don't serve a Reuben sandwich here. I would love one of those."

"Rubens has to be grilled. I don't have a grill."

"You don't have a deep fryer, either."

"Oh please, we just had this conversation." Paige groaned. "Just give me my sandwich and let me eat in peace."

"So Jimmy got himself shot," Irwin said, starting to make one of the sandwiches. "Can't say I am not surprised. He was a jerk, especially in high school. His old man do it."

"I have my doubts," Abby said, watching him make the sandwich. "You're kind of scrimping on the pastrami there."

"You want extra pastrami? Just ask."

"No, I want the usual amount of pastrami," Abby said, looking over the display case. "I forgot you knew Jimmy. Did you kill him?"

"Is that what you call investigating?" Irwin asked, looking more amused than annoyed.

"Yes, if I ask enough people, someone will say yes. That would make my life so much easier. If you said yes, I could have Paige arrest you, and I could eat my lunch, thinking I just earned my paycheck."

"Sadly for you, I didn't do it," Irwin said, putting her sandwich on the counter. "Here's your sandwich. Catsup is on the table. But seriously, any idea who did it?"

"No clue, but the state has dumped in her lap," Paige said, leaning over and watching Irwin make her sandwich. "They figure someone in town did it, so Abby gets to play detective."

"Play detective," Irwin said, laughing. "I like that. I will have to tell the wife."

"You know, I haven't signed off on your promotion and raise yet," Abby said, picking up her sandwich and walking off.

"She is just joking," Paige said, taking her sandwich from Irwin. "She'll sign off."

"You know who you should talk to," Irwin said, pointing his finger at Paige. Hershel is down at the sports bar. He was close to Jimmy back in the day."

"Back in the day? That is my first time hearing someone use that phrase in real life. But thanks for the tip. French fries would be good, though."

"Go!" Irwin snapped, pointing at Abby across the room.

CHAPTER 23

"Good afternoon, ladies," Shaun said, looking up from his computer. His fingers kept dancing across the keyboard. "Two calls. A Walt from the state police was driving down and requested you wait for him. Something about reports. Merry Jo called. Said she needed to speak to you about the murder."

"Thank you, Shaun," Abby said, walking over to the coffee pot and pouring herself a cup. She took a sip and looked up. "Wow, this is delicious coffee. Got a real snap to it. Well done, Shaun. I would give you a raise, but I did just hire you."

"Why thank you, Sheriff. I aim to please," he said with a smile. "I saw Lionel wandering around the park again, looking creepy. It looked like he was debating on whether to come in or not. Just thought you would want to know."

"Thanks. I think Lionel had been peeping into windows again. Tell everyone, and this time, no warning. Just arrest him. He is now officially, as you put it, on the creepy list. Oh, Shaun, did you know that Bobby Huston was gay?"

"Best kept secret in town," he said with a laugh. "Except for those of us in the know. He dated Allison May and never got into her panties. Please. If I had not been gay, I would have tried to get her into her panties. I bet she has some nice ones, too."

"That would interest you," Abby asked. "I mean, what kind of panties does she wear?"

"Only because I have some friends who are into that."

"Here in town?" Abby asked, stepping closer.

"Like I would tell you," Shaun said, looking amused.

"I am your boss."

"Only when it comes to law and order in our fair city. My private life and those of my friends are none of your concern."

"Wow, maybe I don't know this town. Maybe I can use that to dump this murder back into Walt's lap."

"I have my doubts. There is a reason why no one has gotten into Allison's sexy panties. I know they are sexy since we had gym class together," Paige said, sitting down at her desk. "Lots of lace and silk."

"Oh please, do tell," Shaun said, leaning forward.

"About the panties?"

"No. Why did no one get into Allison's panties? We'll discuss the other matter when the boss isn't around."

"I can still fire you two," Abby said, returning to the coffee and frowning. "We need to start bringing in cookies...cookies with chocolate."

"Fine," said Shaun. "I bake some tonight. Now spill!"

"Money. Allison May couldn't take the chance of losing all that money. If she had an accident and said accident produced a son, the son got the money."

"So she is still..."

"That's what she says," Abby said. "Turns out Allison May is a lot smarter than we were led to believe. And has a lot more willpower and discipline than I thought was possible. I don't have a motive for her, but she is still on my list."

They all looked up when a tall, older man entered the office. He had to be a little over six feet, with a lean body of muscle from work, not the gym. His skin was tanned from being outside. He had the hands of a man who knew hard work. His hair and thick mustache were snow white, but he looked younger than his hair would make you think. His bright blue eyes sparkled like he had just told a clever joke. There were laugh lines around his eyes. He wore black jeans, a red flannel shirt, and round-toed cowboy boots. He held two large duffle bags and a padded rifle case in one hand. He smiled and nodded before he spoke. "Afternoon, ladies and sir, or should I be calling you officers? I am new in town."

"Abby or Sheriff is fine. Whatever you are comfortable with." Abby crossed the room and extended her hand. She had an odd feeling about this man. "Those are my deputies: Page Walton and Shaun."

"Shaun doesn't have a last name?" he asked, taking her hand and giving it a firm shake - which scored points with the sheriff.

"Apparently not," Shaun said, sounding offended. "You are new in town. I would remember meeting you."

"Small town," Abby said, glaring at Shaun. "So, what brings you to Digger's Cove with a rifle? Hunting season is not for three months."

"Oh, this," he said with a grin, lifting the rifle case up. "I don't use this for hunting. This is an 1873 Winchester in perfect condition. Handed down from father to son over the years. If you believe my great granddaddy, he won this in a card game from Doc Holiday."

"Well, if you believe the movies and TV, Doc was a gambler but preferred pistols."

"That he did, but used a shotgun at the OK Corral shootout," He said with a grin. "But I am not one to call my great granddaddy a liar. Oh, mind my manners. My name is Sam Ellis, and you apparently have my bike."

"So you are the owner of the Harley," Abby said with a smile and sighed. "Sadly, I don't have your bike. The state police do."

"Actually, we do have it," Shaun said. Rather than hauling it back to state headquarters, they covered it with plastic and stuck it in our storage locker out back."

"Well, thank you for the update," Abby said, giving him a look that suggested he should have told her sooner. 'Still, it is evidence in a murder investigation. It belongs to the state."

"But Sheriff, you are leading the investigation," Paige said, trying to look helpful. Couldn't you..."

"No, I can't." Abby glared this time at Paige, turning her attention back to Sam. When she saw Paige's interest in the newcomer, she decided to have some fun. She smiled. "Good help is hard to find. But the state investigator is coming in this afternoon; I could speak to him."

"That would be just fine, Sheriff," Sam said with a big grin. "I don't mind hanging around for a day or two. Maybe longer. Give me a chance to get a better look at some of the cars in town. I have never seen so many vintage cars in such excellent condition in one place - and being driven."

"Do you like vintage cars?" Paige said, moving closer with a big smile. Everyone has one. I have a bright red '55 T-bird."

"I would love to see that."

"Sadly, it's not here, but it's parked in my garage, under a car cover, of course."

"I am sure Mr. Ellis would love to see your car," Abby said, giving Paige a cool look. But if he is staying in town, he needs to get settled. Would you prefer renting a room or going to a hotel?"

"A hotel? I didn't see one coming into town."

"Oh, it's not a major chain. It's run by Hank and Mable Stewart. Big rooms, clean sheets, and towels. They have cable. You noticed your phone won't work here.

"We have no tower," Paige said, moving right by Sam with a huge smile. All the phone companies decided it wasn't worth the expense to put up a tower here."

"I don't have a wireless phone," he said with another small smile. "Never saw the need. So everyone in this town has a landline?"

"Mostly." Abby gave Paige another smile. "The kids have them, but they don't work until they reach the main road. We do have the internet, just not wireless."

"Ladies, I think I may have died and gone to Heaven," Sam said. "You may have to pick me up. I am not a big fan of technology. Apparently, there is nothing to do until this state cop gets here. So if you can point me in the right direction of the hotel..."

"Allow me to show you," Abby said, taking Sam's elbow and leading him to the door. "It's time for my patrol of the town."

"Lucy is on patrol," Paige said, her eyes sharp and mean.

"Backup," Abby said, hustling Sam out the door. Once she had him out, she stuck her tongue out at her deputy.

Paige mouthed the word "bitch."

CHAPTER 24

"I appreciate this, Sheriff," Sam said, standing on the sidewalk. He turned and looked at the '55 Chevy police car. "You got a sweet ride, Sheriff."

"It actually belongs to the city. Sadly, it's a stick," Abby said, moving beside the man.

"You don't like a stick?"

"No, too much work. I am lazy when it comes to driving. My father was so ashamed."

"I don't think so," he said with a smile and shook his head. He looked at the red Corvette parked in front of the cop car and moved down. Sam squatted down and rubbed the damage on the fender. "Now, that is a shame. Not too bad. It can be buffed out. The paint will be the problem. You could get by painting just the fender, but it never matches. If I were doing the repairs, I would suggest repainting the whole car. But that's me."

"You work on cars?"

"Yes, I do," Sam said, standing up and smiling. "Not the new ones. Old ones like this. Contrary to what you see on reality TV, I am a dying breed. Just had to close my shop in Vegas. You would think Vegas would have an overabundance of old cars. Sadly, no. I was about to sell the Harley before it was borrowed."

"So you are unemployed?" Abby asked, now interested.

"Unemployed and homeless. I sold my house, too. Got a good price for it and the business, so I am not destitute. I was selling the Harley because I didn't want to haul it around, and my truck gave up the ghost. But as they say, bad luck comes in threes. Still trying to figure out what number I'm up to now. I had nothing in Vegas. So I put all my stuff in storage and took the bus here to get the bike. I was going to fly, but apparently, it is faster to take the bus."

"That might be true," Abby said with a smile. "I don't know if you would be interested, but the man who does bodywork in this town is getting ready to retire. That's one of the reasons this 1955 Corvette is just sitting here and not in the shop."

"Sheriff, like I said. I may have died and gone to Heaven. Let's get my bags stowed at the hotel, and then I can go around and have a chat with this fellow. You can give me directions."

"I can do better than that," Abby said, going to the trunk of her car and opening it. Put your bags in here. I'll take you to the hotel and drive you to see Henry."

"Why, Sheriff, you are being more than helpful. I do appreciate it."

"Actually, that's the mayor's car. I am just trying to score points."

"Still, I may just have to buy you dinner."

"Well, I won't say no," Abby said, kicking herself. She was taking this joke too far. She was actually leading this poor man on. Of course, the town would need someone to do bodywork on their cars.

CHAPTER 25

As Abby walked into the sheriff's station, Shaun looked up but didn't stop typing. Paige looked up from the report she was filling out. "You bitch!"

"What?" Abby said, trying to look innocent as she got some coffee. "I am just being friendly."

"Friendly?" Paige stood and approached her boss. "I had to mop up the drool off the floor. Didn't you see I was interested?"

"Oh, were you?" Abby said, heading for her office.

"Don't go hide in your office. You used your rank to block me out. You should have backed off when you saw I was interested."

Shaun stopped typing to watch the two women as if he were watching a tennis match.

"Wait, are you saying I was obligated to back off because you showed interest in Sam?" Abby asked. "I don't think how it works. Now, I will admit, I am not up on the latest dating etiquette, but I am pretty sure Paige getting first shot at all desirable males is not a rule."

"It has been years since you showed interest in any man."

"Maybe I have been waiting for the right man," Abby lied.

"Fine, since we both appear to be interested in the same man, I suggest we stay on polite terms. Keep it professional while working together."

"I have no problem with that," Abby said, turning back to her office door. Two things I feel should be shared: One, he may be moving here and taking over Henry's body shop."

"Thank you for sharing," Paige said with a sarcastic tone.

"The plot thickens," Shaun said. "And the other thing?"

"We may be having dinner tonight," Abby said. Then she ducked into her office and quickly closed the door.

"Abby!" Paige yelled and tried to open the door. She looked back at Shaun. "She locked the door. She actually locked the door. You can't stay in there forever! Abby!"

Lucy walked into the station, stopped, and watched Paige bang on Abby's door. She moved over by Shaun. "I miss something?"

"New guy in town," Shaun said, still watching Paige.

"Sam?" Lucy smiled. I just met him. He's a nice guy. He was going into the bank. He's thinking of moving here."

"Oh God, not you, too," Shaun said with a groan. "This could turn into a soap opera. Worse. You all carry guns."

"Abby doesn't care a gun," Lucy said.

"She's got one and knows how to use it," he said.

"There is that." Lucy nodded. "For the record, I am not interested. It's a little old for me. But Megan, who works at the bank, sure looked interested."

"Megan?" Paige asked, turning from the door. "Are you sure?"

"Yes, I was walking by and met Sam," Lucy said. "We got to talking, and Megan walked up. She was just coming back from lunch. Sam notices her. He makes the same remark everyone makes about her looking like a redhead from that TV show MAD MEN. Instead of rolling her eyes, she touches his arm and laughs. Fake laugh, but still Megan, not known for her great sense of humor. She takes him into the bank by the arm with the biggest smile. I think she giggled at something Sam said. I don't remember Megan ever giggling."

"God damn, that bitch," Paige snarled.

"So anyone interested in the new guy is a bitch?" Shaun said, turning back to his keyboard. "I will tell you this: there really aren't enough eligible men in this town. It is really quite a shame he isn't gay. So I am confused."

"What? You too?" Paige asked.

"Paige, relax. He doesn't play on my team. But trust me, Sam will be the most popular guy in town by this time next week. As I said, this town has a real shortage of Bachelors. "

"Good for him," Lucy said, walking over to the coffee pot and pouring herself a cup. "The best part is I get to watch. Oh, Head Deputy? I think Lionel is peeping into the windows again. Mrs. Lawry, who leaves her curtains open while doing yoga, is sure she saw him looking through her window."

"Is she still doing it in the nude?" Paige asked, returning to her desk and sitting. She began to nervously twirl a pen in her hand.

"That's why she leaves the curtains open," Lucy said. "At least, that's what I think. Maybe I will tell Sam about it. She does have a nice body."

"Yoga does help," Shaun said, starting to type again. "At least, that's what I hear."

"You know, Lucy, I am your boss," Paige said.

"My lips are sealed, but he will find out," Lucy said. Mrs. Lawry wants people to see her doing yoga in the buff—apparently everyone but Lionel."

"About Lionel. No more warnings," Paige said. "We catch him, we arrest him."

"Ladies, I am confused," Shaun said. "I thought the sheriff..."

"Shaun, don't," Paige said. "And only mention Merry Jo if it is job-related."

"Ah, still confused."

"Pretty much everyone in town is," Lucy said.

Walt entered the office and smiled. "I am here to see the sheriff."

"Let me get her out here for you," Paige said, jumping up and going to Abby's. She banged on the door with her fist. "Sheriff, state police are here!"

CHAPTER 26

Abby smiled as she walked around her desk, ignoring Paige. It was fun to pull her strings from time to time, but she had no real interest in Sam.

Why wasn't she interested? He was handsome, tall, and, as they say, a man's man. Why wasn't he? Her type? What was her type?

Merry Jo?

Now, she wanted to talk to her about the case?

She slumped in her chair and stared at the index cards and crude drawing. "Why did you stop, Jimmy?"

The sheriff sipped her coffee, thinking she really needed some cookies. Then she focused on the problem at hand—the murder. Jimmy would stop if Kirk or Allison May were standing in the middle of the road.

But...

She couldn't see Allison May standing in the middle of the road. It just didn't seem to be her style. Abby could see the town beauty queen poisoning Jimmy, but shooting him in the face? Too messy. Could Kirk even get out of the house without Nancy knowing? The only thing she had found out was Allison May was now rich. She already knew Kirk James's family had money. It would be interesting to know if Keanu had money. She was pretty sure Lizzie Eastbourne had no money to speak of. You don't get rich working as a cocktail waitress.

"Sure as there is a God, Jimmy was coming back for money," Abby said. "What was your plan, Jimmy? The days of you sweet-talking the ladies were done. Blackmail, probably. But you don't blackmail the James family. Allison May probably had some powerful lawyers to hide behind. Was Lionel mixed up in this? Remember Abby, Jimmy was not known for his brains. What he thought was a brilliant plan could have been stupid. "Oh, Jimmy, why couldn't you get yourself killed someplace else."

Annoyed, Abby looked over at the door when Paige banged. Was she really that interested in Sam? Was it just because he was the new guy in town? It looked like Sam was staying here in Digger's Cove. Abby's future was in New York, or that was what she kept telling herself.

"Give it a rest," Abby muttered when Paige banged again. Then she heard the words state police. Groaning, she got up and opened the door. "Hi Walt, you can come in. You too, Paige. Please tell me you got something."

"Yes, I do," Walt said, holding a file. "Let's get some coffee."

"So you don't have the name of the murderer?"

"That would be a no," Walt said with a grin as he poured himself some coffee, sipped it, and smiled. "This is delicious coffee."

"Thank you," Shaun said with a smile. "We will be serving Hawaiian roast and cookies tomorrow. Maybe chocolate chip, but those are so cliché. I want to make something interesting."

"Well, since you have a dead body," Walt said, walking over to Abby and holding up a notebook. "I have an excuse to come back. Do you want to explain how so many rich people ended up in Digger's Cove? I had no idea."

"How many?" Lucy asked, looking up from her own computer. She ignored the glare from Abby. "I am just asking. I am part of the investigating team."

"I guess you are," Abby said with a shrug. "We may as well stay out here."

"That's where the coffee is," Walt said, flipping through his notebook. "Oh yes, an agent from the FBI called me. Asked really politely to keep him updated on the investigation."

"FBI?" Abby asked. "What the hell is going on?"

"I don't know," Walt said and continued. "I assume you know about the James family. I ran a check on Kirk James. Less than an hour later, a lawyer from New York called me and asked why I was running the check. I told him. Then he told me – not asked, told me – to keep him in the loop. Anyone else I would have complained, but that family is richer than God."

"And as a state investigator, you thought it best to keep them in the loop," Abby said. "I am starting to believe the James family would have no problem hiring someone to kill Jimmy."

"Oh, they wouldn't have any problem with that, but Jimmy's murder was public," Walt said.

"So they would be more of the making Jimmy just disappear?" Paige asked.

"Yes." Walt looked back at his notes. "Now, you may not know this, but Allison May Towns just came into a whole lot of money. To be fair, she has just a little over four hundred million in cash and owns property in New York, Beverly Hills, and Miami. Altogether, she is worth a cool billion."

"We found that out this morning. Did you say a billion?" Abby said, looking surprised.

"Yes."

"Wow, that is a lot of money," Abby said.

"That face, that body, and now a billion bucks," Paige said. "Some people are just born lucky."

"Why are these two here?" Walt asked. "I mean, no disrespect to your town, but shouldn't they be living in Los Angeles or New York or any number of places that rich people live?"

"Allison May had no choice," Paige said. "Her great-granddaddy was born here. He used to own most of the town. Maybe Allison May now owns most of the town. But he put it all into a trust. It was required that the family live here until they graduated high school. Something to do with keeping them humble. But now she's got the money. She is leaving and moving to New York. Probably going to live in one of her own buildings."

"Kirk's parents moved here after the kids were born," Abby said. "They wanted to raise their children in a small town. Sadly, Kirk had mental issues, so he stays here."

"Mental problems?" Walt asked.

"I know what you are thinking. I don't think its Kirk," Abby said. "He never leaves his house. He just went to Vegas, which was huge for him."

"Well, I hope it is not him," Walt said. "I really don't want to annoy the James family. Now Keanu Watershaw is interesting. Do you know his IQ and multiple degrees are off the charts? He is a resident professor and consultant for Oregon Tech. Whatever that is. He doesn't teach classes but did invent some kind of gizmo for computers that he sold to a big company for a hundred million..."

"Keanu is worth a hundred million!" Lucy gasped. "I will have to start being nicer to him."

"That answers a lot of questions," Paige said.

"What questions?" Walt asked.

"How he is paying for all his experiments," Abby said. "He has a lab back in the hills. We've had complaints, but then the complaints were dropped."

"Probably paid them off," Lucy said. "Ben Petersen got that new truck last year."

"Someone bought a new truck in this town?" Walt asked.

"New for this town," Abby said. "1958 Chevy Cameo. Beautiful truck. They were hard to find, so it wasn't cheap. Why don't you come out with Paige and me? We are going to have a chat with Keanu."

"Sure, why not," Walt said. "This Elizabeth Eastbourne is anything but rich. Local waitress. Maxed out on her credit cards and twenty bucks in the bank. Not sure why she is on the list. Now, this local artist is rich. Not on the level of the others, but she just sold a statue for a cool million. She could live somewhere else, but artists and writers are weird. Lastly is this Lionel character. According to the internet, he doesn't exist. There is a birth certificate. After that, nothing. No driver's license, checking, savings accounts, or credit cards. He appears to have never made any money but now rents a small house. I could ruin his life by telling the IRS he has never filed a tax return. I mean, never."

"If you knew Lionel," Abby said, "you would not be surprised by all that. It's not a house, closer to a cabin...or a really nice shack. Aside from the money. Do you have anything?"

"They all have clean backgrounds. No arrests, DUIs, or anything that would say this person is your murderer. Kirk has a lot of medical expenses, but we need a court order to get a look."

"And the James family will ensure we don't," Paige said.

"That would be my guess," Walt said with a shrug. "One interesting thing. Allison May only left town for beauty pageants and other related events. However, while visiting Los Angeles, she had a medical procedure. She paid cash, so I guess she was trying to keep it quiet."

"Medical Procedure?" Lucy asked. "That could be anything. Any idea what it was?"

"We need a court order to find that out too," Walt said. "No judge will give us one without cause."

"I can only think of the surgeries Allison May wouldn't want known," Paige said, "That would be cosmetic. The pageants probably frown on that. "

"No. Everything about Allison is natural. God was so good to her," Shaun said, looking up. "As for the pageants, it is like the army: don't ask or tell. Publicly, the pageants frown on it but don't care. They want ratings, which gets them sponsors. Which gets them money. They want perfect beauty with amazing bodies. I had a friend who competed back in the day. She told me stuff. A lot of those beauty queens are not nice people. A lot of backstabbing going on. She dropped out because it just got too expensive. It takes a lot of money to become Miss America. God knows how much it takes to become Miss Universe."

Abby rubbed her chin like she was deep in thought. "I can think of one thing that Allison May wouldn't want known. For two good reasons. I have my doubts that an abortion would win you any crowns."

"Are you suggesting Allison May isn't what she claims?" Paige asked, looking more thrilled than she should.

"Careful," Shaun said. "Allison May can be quite the bitch. Her being a virgin could explain that."

"Allison May claims to be a virgin?" Walt asked. "The redhead with that...great body?"

"We have to stop right now," Abby said. "I was just thinking out loud. We have no proof. We might not ever get proof. To be honest, since Allison May has so much money, we really don't want to piss her off until we get proof."

"So what do we do?" Paige asked.

"Lucy goes back on patrol. And we go talk to Keanu."

CHAPTER 27

"So, what is the deal with this guy?" Walt asked as they walked up a winding path up a small hill. A long, wide metal building with a slanted Gable roof. It was unpainted, so the rust and other signs of age were evident. Twin doors were open at one end. The building had no windows. A colossal dumpster sat at the back. It was filled with metal scraps and junk. "He's got a hundred million and is living in a one-bedroom. A very nice, clean one-bedroom, but still. The lawn is well-tended, and a peek through the window told me the place is clean. I am guessing he has a cleaning lady and a gardener. What kind of car does he drive?"

"He doesn't drive. He rides a bike," Abby said, moving toward the open doors. "Keanu is very green, and you know the old saying. There is a fine line between genius and insanity. He is on the line. For the last two years, he has been obsessed with time."

They walked into the building and stopped. There was a small setup, like a living area. There was a sofa, recliner, coffee table, and fridge. There was a counter holding a top-of-the-line coffee/tea maker. A microwave. A large trash can sat in the corner. It was almost overflowing with food containers and Pizza boxes. But what caught the eye was the time machine sitting farther back in the room. It looked like an exact duplicate of the old movie. Velvet chair, brass railing, and a giant spinning disc. The three lights in front were blinking. Behind it was a heavy steel wall with a door that looked like it belonged on a WW2 submarine? The words KEEP OUT were spray painted on the wall.

"Wow, he built a time machine?" Walt said, moving closer to the time machine and smiling. "My old man loved that movie. I only watched it because the blonde actress was really hot. Turned out to be a pretty good movie. You think this works?"

The metal door opened. A tall, thin man wearing a flannel shirt, jeans, and high-end Nikes emerged. His long black hair hung just past his ears. He was clean-shaven with a narrow but pleasant face. Round, gold, wire-framed glasses rested on his nose. He was in his thirties but looked younger, and he appeared startled to find people in his lab. "Whoa! How did you get in here? This a secure location."

"You left the doors open again, Keanu," Abby said, walking over and smiling. If you want to keep this place secure, you have to close the doors and turn on the security system."

"Yeah, yeah, you are right, Sheriff," He looked over at Walt and snapped, "Don't touch that!"

"Work in progress?" Walt asked with a smile.

"It doesn't work. It cost me a fortune to have it made down in Los Angeles. I could have done the work myself, but no time. No time. It is for inspiration. Then I will have all the time in the world," Keanu said, rubbing his hands together nervously. "All the time in the world. The real one is back in the lab."

"You built a real-time machine?" Walt said, looking really interested. Are you planning on going back in time or to the future?"

"You can't go back in time!" he snapped.

"Oh God, here we go," Paige groaned.

"You saw that movie," Keanu said in a dismissive tone. "That is not how nanotechnology works. As if. All that nonsense about timelines and such. Nonsense. You can't go back in time because it is set. We are standing here as a result of events from the past. Those events can't be changed. There is no Butterfly Effect. But!"

"Here it comes," Abby said, going to the coffee maker. It was one of the modern kinds that used pods. She started to go through the pods, smiled, and put one in the machine.

"We can go into the future. That is not set. The possibilities are endless. Once perfected, I will go into the future and obtain future technology that I will bring back." He frowned. "If they will let me."

"So you can go into the future and then return to the past?" Walt asked. "But..."

"Only to the point when I left," Keanu said. You think I am mad. Come, I will show you."

Abby finished making her coffee and looked over. "You really going to show us this time?"

"Why not? Yes, why not!" Keanu said, looking very excited. He stepped through the door and waved them to follow him. "It's time you see the results of my hard work...and my genius."

"Oh boy," Abby said, following Keanu through the door. She sipped her coffee. "Good coffee."

"Thank you, it's a new flavor. I like it." Keanu looked back with a smile but kept moving forward.

They came into the workshop that filled the rest of the building. A long table had four computers set up. Each one had two monitors. Four of the screens were filled with numbers moving back and forth. The rest of the monitors were logged into what looked like science sites. The last one was tuned to YouTube. A band with a blonde was singing about her relationship being over. There were other worktables cluttered with tools, electronics, and metal parts. A raised platform was at the very back of the lab. A strange device was floating a few inches off the floor. A chair with a small control panel was encircled by two gold hoops. The hoops slowly rotated around the chair. There was a black box mounted behind the chair. The box gave off a faint blue glow while green lights on the top blinked. They all walked forward and stared at the floating device.

"It's floating," Page said, looking confused. "How..."

"A magnetic field," Keanu said with a smile, rubbing his hands together. "The government would love to get their hands on this. Maybe if I run low on funds... No! No! They will turn it into a weapon. That would be bad."

"That's not going to happen anytime soon," Walt said, moving around the strange device. I mean, we're running low on funds."

"Speaking of money," Abby said, remembering why they were here. "Did you hear about Jimmy Evans?"

"Jimmy Evan? Jimmy Evans? Jimmy Evans. I don't know the name." Then his face brightened. "Oh yes, the bully from high school. I didn't like him. Used to take my money. But he won't be taking my money again."

"Why won't he be taking your money?" Abby asked.

"Oh, perfected my blaster."

"You made a blaster, like from Star Wars?" Walt asked.

"Yes...well, theoretically." Keanu approached a counter and held up what looked like a blaster from the movie, except this one had a cable coming out the bottom of the handle. The cable ran to a small silver box sitting on the floor. "I haven't had the chance to field test it. Do you think the military might be interested in this? But I would need to make sure it worked. I just want it to stun people, not kill them."

Abby stepped forward, raising one hand when Keanu started to aim the weapon. "Keanu, now might not be the time."

"It should work. The science is sound," Keanu said, looking at the pistol. "I could try it now."

"No, no, no," Abby said, coming even closer and carefully pushing Keanu's hand down so the barrel of the blaster was pointed at the floor. She looked a little afraid and then smiled. "You want to only stun. The army? Not interested so much in just stunning people."

"It should work, but you are right about killing."

"I am sure it does." Abby sounded nervous but managed to get him to put the weapon down. "The reason we are here is because Jimmy was killed outside of town. Shot with a pistol."

"I don't have a pistol. I have this," Keanu said, bringing up the blaster again and then frowning. "Wait. Wait. Someone called. A man. Yes, a man. He wanted money, or he would tell the government about my experiments. I would prefer they not know about my time machine. Wait! Wait! I was in Las Vegas a few months back. It was a conference for scientists like myself."

"Scientists like you?" Paige asked, still looking at the device.

"Scientists like me. Who. What is the phrase? Scientists who think outside the box. Some rude fellow kept following me around, acting like he knew me. That could have been Jimmy. Older, smelled like he'd been drinking."

"Did he ask you for money?" Abby asked.

"Yes, he did. As if I would give him any. Not in grade school anymore," Keanu said, lost in thought. Then he smiled. Now that you are all here, you will be my witnesses." He ran over to one of the computers and started to type. "This is a prototype, and I will lose it if my experiment is successful."

"You are going to send it through time?" Walt said, stepping back when the twin loops began to twirl around even faster. The machine started to give a low humming sound that slowly became louder. A dull blue glow engulfed the machine.

Abby and the rest stepped back. The entire building began to shake, which made her look up. She noticed the new roof panels. Lots of new roof panels. The Sheriff looked at Keanu. "Keanu, have you done this experiment before?"

"Yes," Keanu said, still typing while watching the screen.

"Successfully?" she asked.

"No."

Abby looked up at the ceiling again. Then, at the shaking walls. Then she remembered the dumpster filled with metal scrapes. She grabbed Paige and Walt and shoved them toward the door. "Run!"

They resisted at first, both fascinated with the spinning, glowing machine. A loud crack snapped them out of it. Then, all three ran out the door. They fled the building and took cover behind some trees.

The entire building was shaking. After a few moments, Keanu ran out and dove under some bushes. There was a loud boom. The machine crashed through the roof and into the air a second later. It hovered for a second before falling down. It crashed outside the building, the once-beautiful machine now just a twisted mass of metal.

Keanu got up and dusted himself off while looking at the wrecked machine. Abby and the others joined him. He glanced at them. "Again. It went straight up instead of through time."

"How many times have you done this?" Abby asked.

"Not sure," he said, looking dazed and sad. "This is my fourth dumpster. I have to call the roofers. Get my roof fixed."

"That explains how Marty could afford the remodel on his house," Paige said.

"Marty fixes roofs?" Walt asked.

"Yes," Paige said.

"I think we can all agree Keanu isn't the murderer," Abby said. "I will be talking to the mayor about this."

"Abby!" Lucy yelled as she walked up the path, stopping when she saw the wrecked machine and hole in the roof. "What the hell happened?"

"Failed experiment," Abby said. "What are you doing here?"

"Tried to call you on the radio," Lucy said. "We got a report of another dead body."

CHAPTER 28

"Well, there goes my number one suspect," Abby said, looking down at the body. The very dead person was lying in the middle of a small living room with a green carpet that may have once been shaggy. The furniture had seen better days, with a sofa and chair that may have been overstuffed with a long-since faded floral print. A round coffee table made of fake wood that seemed to be lopsided. A TV with rabbit ears sat on a stand made of cinder blocks and boards. A metal desk that belonged in an office cubical sat in one corner. Most of the surface was cluttered with books, magazines, and papers set up in one corner. The walls were bare except for a huge poster of Allison May in her birthday suit. It looked like she was walking out of the bathroom.

The Sheriff sighed and squatted down beside Lionel. His white polo shirt was red with blood, and his eyes and mouth were wide open. "Well, Lionel, did you peek in the wrong window?"

"He looks shocked," Paige said, squatting beside her boss.

"I'll call my lab boys," Walt said. "We should back out here now."

"I tell you this," Lucy said, looking down. "Those holes were not made by a twenty-two. Thirty-eight at least."

"People, let's go," Walt said. "You're screwing up my crime scene."

Abby looked up with a smile. "Does that mean you are taking back the case?" Then she frowned. Then, still squatted down, she duck-walked over to the desk and looked under it. Then she stood up and took a quick look at the desk. There was a clear spot in the middle of the desk. Then she saw the pistol. "Well, I got a surge protector and an open spot for a laptop. So Lionel had a computer. And have what looks like a Walther P22."

"What!" Walt and Paige rushed over, staring down at the pistol.

"I could be wrong, but that looks like a suppressor lying beside it," Abby said. "Careful, you don't want to mess up your crime scene."

"Your crime scene," Walt said, pulling out his cell phone. "You just demonstrated why I am letting you handle it."

"It won't work here," Abby said with a sigh. "I just read too many murder mysteries. Everyone out. My crime scene. You can use the radio in the car."

"Playboy?" Lucy asked, looking down at the stack of magazines. "Not surprised Lionel read it. But I didn't know that was still a thing. Didn't he just die?"

"Hefner died," Abby said, waving her hands to make everyone move outside. "The magazine lives on.

The small group moved outside. Lucy took Walt to her car. Paige and Abby stood on the porch of the small house. It had seen better days. The paint was faded and cracking, and the lawn was mostly dirt and weeds. When the porch groaned under their feet, they stepped off.

"What do you think this means?" Paige asked.

"It means we may have two killers," Abby said, looking down at her boots. Then she looked up. "I am betting the pistol on the desk will turn out to be the pistol that killed Jimmy. The question is, did Lionel use it, or was it planted here? Did Lionel have a partner? Did this partner double-cross Lionel? Or is the real killer trying to make Lionel the fall guy? But the big question is, why is Lionel dead? We figure that out, and we will have our killer. Maybe for both murders."

"That makes sense," Paige said. "We know Lionel was a peeper. Maybe he saw something he shouldn't have...or took a picture of something he shouldn't have. That poster was a blowup. You can tell he took it through the window. Wait, didn't you know Lionel was holding back something?"

"Yeah, I should have pushed him harder," Abby said. "That poster is too big to make on a computer...he had it done somewhere. What was Lionel using the computer for? He doesn't have cable. Probably no Internet, either."

"I am guessing," Page said, "he had a ton of pictures on it."

"Obviously, there was something on the computer the killer didn't want us to see," Abby said, pacing.

"That could explain why the computer is gone," Paige said.

"God, we should have busted Lionel a long time ago. Then he and Jimmy might both still be alive."

"That's stretch," Lucy said.

"How close were Lionel and Jimmy?" Abby asked. "We all assumed that Lionel hung around Jimmy to avoid getting bullied. What if they were really friends? We need to check his phone calls and see who he has been calling. Like you said, the killer took the computer for a reason. Why?"

"Like I said, there was something on it that he didn't want us to see," Paige said. "Hey, I saw Lionel posting a letter. Maybe he was using snail mail?"

"We need to get back in there," Abby said, turning as Walt walked up.

"They are on their way," Walt said, looking over Abby's face. "What?"

"I need to get in there," Abby said. "Lionel wrote letters. The name of the killer could be in there."

"No, we have to protect the chain of evidence. My crime scene guys will be here in less than an hour. I will tell them to look for letters first. You have an idea. What is it?"

"I have nothing to back this up. Lionel was a peeping Tom. Now we know he was taking pictures and writing to someone. Let's say he was writing Jimmy. Lionel sees something and tells Jimmy about it. Jimmy sees it as a way to make some money. Comes back. I bet you Lionel knew he was coming back."

"Maybe Lionel did kill him?" Paige said. "Jimmy would stop for Lionel, his old buddy."

"Jimmy and the dead guy were buddies?" Walt asked.

"We are guessing," Abby replied. "I need to get into that house. I need to...I need to...I need to know why Lionel was killed. He found out something. Something that got him killed."

"Someone's secret that they didn't want to be known," Paige said.

"A secret worth killing for," Walt said.

"The question is, who in Digger's Cove has that kind of secret?"

CHAPTER 29

"God, I knew it," Abby said, reading a piece of notebook paper inside an evidence bag. "He was writing Jimmy. Keeping him updated on what was happening."

"Why would Jimmy care?" Paige asked, looking at another plastic-wrapped letter.

"Maybe he wanted to come home," Walt said, looking at another letter. "It's a big, mean world out there. He wasn't doing well. Trouble comes; most people run home."

"These letters read like two pen pals," Abby said, frowning. "I am getting the impression that Jimmy had very few friends. Even bullies get lonely. Now, I am kind of feeling sorry for Jimmy. Maybe he was just coming home to come home. Maybe even make amends."

"He does sound kind of depressed in these letters," Paige said. "Wow, Jimmy does sound kind of lost."

"Looks like they exchanged letters once a month," Abby said, looking through several bagged letters. She goes back and forth. "We're missing the last three months. Lionel got rid of them."

"Or his killer took them," Walt said. "I tell you, this smells like a frame job. A bad one, but I think someone is trying to blame the murder on the town weirdo."

"Maybe they didn't mean to kill him," Abby said, thumbing the letters. "I can see Jimmy blackmailing someone, but Lionel? I am not seeing it. I know this: the two murders are connected. I don't need your lab to tell me that is the murder weapon on the desk."

Lucy walked up and waited. "Sheriff, Shaun just radioed in. A solicitor is waiting for you at the Sheriff's office."

"A solicitor?" Paige asked.

"A lawyer," Abby said. "There is a lawyer from England in my office. Can this day get any better?"

Abby paced around for a second and then stopped. "Paige, I need you to go over and tell Allison May she can't leave town. She objects, arrest her."

"I can do that," Paige said with a big smile.

"Lucy, stay here and report anything they find," Abby said. "Walt, can you give me a ride back to the station. Let's go see what this lawyer wants."

CHAPTER 31

"Jeffery Sinclair, of Sinclair, Hastings, and Bartholomew," an older man said, taking off his bowler hat, bowing his head, and extending his hand smoothly. He was wearing a tan vest suit with a shirt starched so stiff it was a miracle he could move his head. The very tasteful black-and-tan tie was knotted into a perfect Windsor knot. His bowler hat and umbrella matched the suit perfectly. His white hair was expertly trimmed, as were his manicured nails. Gold-rimmed glasses sat on his large nose. His brown eyes reflected intellection. The smallest of smiles came to his lips. "As I informed your deputy, I am a solicitor from England. London, to be exact. I am here to discuss a rather delicate matter. As the local law official, I assume you know Elizabeth Eastbourne?"

"Lizzie?" Abby said, taking in the man's attire and thinking of that old British spy show her father loved. The main character was always impeccably dressed. Nothing out of place, even after a fight. Most men watched for the beautiful redhead who could kick anyone's ass but was always getting tied up in some way. "Yeah, the waitress down at Marty's. You're here to see her?"

"Oh my god!" Shaun said, jumping up, looking both surprised and excited. Are you about to tell us that Lizzie is royalty? The plane crash! I just connected now! We all owe Lizzie an apology. Oh, I guess we have to call her Elizabeth now."

"I assume you follow the royal families?" Sinclair asked with a nod. "Your deputy is right. Last month, the entire Eastbourne family was killed on a plane flight to Australia. We have spent the last month tracking down the heirs to the family title and fortune."

"And would that be Lizzie...I mean, Elizabeth?" Abby asked, slumping against a desk and shaking her head.

"Actually, that would be Lady Elizabeth."

"Okay," Abby said, looking up. "Why are you here telling me this instead of Liz...I mean, Lady Elizabeth? I assume there is a reason, maybe a problem with another possible heir?"

"She is the legitimate heir," Sinclair said. "She is entitled to the title and money."

"How much money are we talking about?" Walt asked.

"I am sorry, sir. That is only something I should discuss with Lady Elizabeth." The Englishman looked at Walt disapprovingly. But I can say it is considerable."

"What's the problem, Mr. Sinclair?" Abby asked. "I have a lot going on right now, so..."

"I understand, Sheriff," he said, looking offended that Abby would even think he was wasting her time. "I just arrived in your small town. A little out of the way, but that aside, I learned you've had two murders in the last few days."

"Jimmy Evans and a young man named Lionel."

"James Evans was the one who contacted us and suggested we look into Lady Elizabeth's heritage. He saved us a lot of work. We even offered him a small reward, which I would give him. We agreed to meet here in town."

"Why meet here?" Abby asked. "You could have just sent the money to his bank account."

"Apparently, Mr. Evans did not have a bank account. He suggested we meet here. He said he had some business to take care of. So when I heard of his death, I was rather concerned. Then I heard of the second murder."

"Lionel? Why would Lionel getting killed concern you?"

"That's the main reason I am here. Elizabeth Eastbourne is the direct heir. She will inherit. But while I was traveling, my firm discovered another very distant heir."

"You are telling Lionel and Lizzie, sorry, Lady Elizabeth, are related?" Shaun asked. "That's crazy."

"Very distantly," Sinclair said. "I doubt they were even aware of the connection. Very distant cousins."

"Wait. Lionel was a man," Walt said. "That's means he would get the title and money."

"Sir, passing inheritance over a woman to a man is no longer legal. I believe it was made illegal around 1929. There is no more. I am the man; I get everything. But there was no will."

"Lionel was entitled to part of the estate," Abby said. "Maybe all the way up to half?"

"No, no," Sinclair said with a shake. "The connection, as I said, was quite distant. Perhaps a million, maybe two."

"I would take a million or two," Walt said.

"That is in English pounds," Abby said with a smile. "So it would closer to two or three million American dollars. So Lionel ending up dead concerns you."

"Yes," he said solemnly.

"I have known Lizzie my entire life..."

"Lady Elizabeth," he corrected.

"Whatever. But the entire town would have heard of it if Elizabeth found out she was really an English royal. Lizzie...Lady Elizabeth couldn't keep a secret if her life depended on it. Plus, small town."

"Very small," Shaun said. "Very few secrets."

"Shaun, I need you to go get...Lady Elizabeth...and bring her here," Abby said. "Don't tell her why. Shaun, I mean it. Don't tell her why. I will fire your ass if you do. I want to see her reaction, and I have a few questions for her ladyship."

CHAPTER 32

"I knew it. I knew it," Lizzie Eastbourne said with a laugh while slapping her knee and tugging down the too-short black skirt she was wearing again. The red blouse was ruffled and tight. Two buttons were undone to give the slightest hint of her bosom. Her bleached blonde hair was pulled up into a messy bun. Her makeup was heavy, lipstick red. The outfit and makeup, she had told Sinclair, increased her tips. All in all, she looked more like a cocktail waitress than Lady Elizabeth.

The fact was, Lizzie might look like what her grandmother would call a floozy. She went to church every Sunday and was always ready to help out with local charity events. As more than one local put it, Lizzie cleaned up really well when not at work.

"Oh, Mr. Sinclair, I am so sorry for my appearance," Lizzie said, suddenly realizing her clothes and makeup. "I work at the local bar and—"

"Lady Eastbourne, I completely understand," Sinclair said with a forced smile. "Once local matters are settled, we can stop in New York and purchase you a new wardrobe."

"Local matters? What are you talking about?" Lizzie asked. "I thought you said I was the heir."

"You are...you are." Sinclair raised both hands to calm her.

"Lizzie?" Abby asked. This got a glare from Lizzie, Sinclair, and Shaun. She ignored them and pushed on. "Did you know Jimmy was coming to town?"

"No, I hardly knew the jerk," Lizzie said, and then, "Oh my, sorry. That was very un-ladylike...I only had a passing acquaintance with Mr. Evans."

"Yeah, right. Jimmy was instrumental in helping Mr. Sinclair's firm find you. He was on his way back here to get his small reward."

"Well then, I am indebted to Mr. Evans," Lizzie said, speaking in a haughty tone. "I would thank him...

"Lizzie…"

"That's Lady Elizabeth," she snapped, even sticking her nose up. It was made worse by Sinclair nodding his approval. Shaun smiling. Walt just rolled his eyes.

"Fine, Lady Elizabeth," Abby said in with a growl. "We now know Jimmy was coming back for his reward. However much that was. He had a notebook on him with your name on it."

"Sheriff," Lizzie said in a tone that made Abby want to punch her. "It is obvious that Mr. Evans was hoping to, how does one put it? Cash in on my good fortune."

"You ain't in England yet, Lizzie," Abby snarled and leaned forward. "I got two dead bodies, and you are one of my suspects. Title or no title. Did you know Jimmy was coming back?"

"No, you know we didn't hang out. Jimmy tried to get into my pants, but that didn't happen." Lizzie waved her hand around her face and body. "This is all for the bar. It pays a lot better than waitressing at the diner. But those days are over. I am going home to wash my face and burn these clothes."

"Not inside the city limits," Shaun said, looking like he was trying to be helpful.

"Did you know you were related to Lionel?" Abby asked.

"Lionel? I am related to the town pervert?" Lizzie asked, looking genuinely surprised.

"Distantly, your ladyship," Sinclair said. "Really not enough to concern yourself with. The firm would have handled the situation for you."

"He would have gotten some money off the estate?"

"Nothing to concern yourself with."

"Two or three million is nothing for her to concern herself with?" Walt asked. "How much money are we talking about?"

"That's none of your damn business," Lizzie snapped. "Who the hell are you?"

"He with the state police," Abby said. "You do know that someone murdered Lionel?"

"Someone shot him. It's about time," Lizzie said. Then she stopped to think and turned to Sinclair. Mr. Sinclair, it occurs to me that I might be a little rough around the edges. I want you to arrange for someone to...what's the word?"

"Educate you so you will present the proper image of being a lady, so you won't embarrass yourself or the title publicly and privately?" Sinclair said with a smile. "Once we have finished our business here, I will make some phone calls. Perhaps, if I may be so bold, we stay in New York for a time so we can purchase your wardrobe and start your lessons."

Lizzie opened her mouth to say something but stopped. Then she put on aloof air and said, "That is an excellent suggestion, Mr. Sinclair. Be so kind as to make the arrangements."

"Consider it done, your ladyship," Sinclair said politely.

"Oh god..." Abby groaned, dropping her head. Then she looked up and forced a smile. "Lady Elizabeth, I am happy for your good fortune, but I will have to insist you remain in town until I clear you of both murders."

"I was helping out at the church when Jimmy was shot. We got Bible School coming up," Lady Elizabeth said with a smug smile. This response seemed to thrill Sinclair by the look he gave his client. "When was Lionel killed? How was he killed?"

Abby looked at Walt, who shrugged and said, "No idea. This is not the movie where you look at the body and know. We have to wait for the coroner's report, but he was definitely shot."

"I saw him yesterday morning," Abby said. "So sometime between that and when we found him. Sometime in the last twenty-four hours. I assume you were working last night until closing."

"The bar closed at two. I was out of there by three," Lady Elizabeth said. "Then I collapsed in bed, got up, ate breakfast at the diner, and went to church. I don't have a gun. You can go over to my place and look if you want."

"Liz..." Abby rolled her eyes. "Lady Elizabeth, I don't think you did it. But I need you to stay in town for a few days. It sounds like you will stay in New York for a while."

"She will need to get a passport," Shaun said. "That takes time."

"I assume Mr. Sinclair will hurry that along," Abby said with a smile.

"You're right, Sheriff," Sinclair said. "But there are phone calls to be made, papers to be signed, and other arrangements for our stay in New York. That will take time. May we leave?"

Abby was about to say yes when the door opened. Paige pulled a handcuffed Allison May into the station. The deputy smiled and said, "She was climbing into her car when I arrived. I told her she couldn't leave town. She objected and took a swing at me."

"You can't do this!" Allison yelled. "I have the right to leave town. Get these off me!"

"Allison May, I got two murders..." Abby said.

"Who else died?" she asked, looking surprised.

"Hey, Lizzie," Paige said. "What's up? Are we still up for coffee tomorrow?"

"That's Lady Elizabeth to you," Shaun said condescendingly.

"What?" Paige asked.

CHAPTER 33

It took almost an hour, including putting Allison in one of the cells, to convince her to stay in town—at least for the next two days. Part of that time was bringing Paige up to date on how one of her friends was now a real English royal. Apparently, they would be drinking tea tonight in celebration of her good fortune.

Finally, Walt left. Paige went with Lady Elizabeth in search of the aforementioned tea. Sinclair had doubts about whether a good cup of tea could be found. Shaun went back to his computer. Abby retreated back to her office with a cup of coffee. It wasn't until she was settled down in her chair that she noticed Allison May standing at her now open door.

"I didn't do it," Allison May said in a deadpan tone.

"I don't think you did, but that's the problem with this town. I don't see anyone being a murderer." Abby leaned back in her chair. "You know I really hate you right now."

"It's your own fault. The way you talk about New York. You make it sound magical."

"New York is like Los Angeles. It is only magical if you have money. And you have money. A lot of money. So you will be fine."

"You could go back with me. I'll even pay for your ticket."

"Allison May, that's sweet of you," Abby said. "Most people don't realize how much I was making at my old job. I was supposed to get married and live the dream. Dad got sick. The dream died a little before Dad did. Going to New York means starting over. I don't know if I have the energy."

"So it's not about money?" Allison May asked. "There are rumors you are sitting on a pile of cash."

"Yes and no. It's complicated."

"Is that complication, Merry Jo?"

"God, there are no secrets in this town."

"Abby, someone started the rumor that you were gay. So that secret is out of the bag, or was it really a secret... Sorry, it's not my business, but if there was a woman I would want to sleep with, it would be Merry Jo."

"She's back to stay, and I don't know how to deal with it."

"Digger's Cove is not your typical small town. Look around, but most people didn't care. Hell, Abby, you got elected despite the rumor and not even making one speech."

"When it comes to Merry Jo, my head is all mixed up. It's like I love and hate her at the same time."

"Or...you love Merry Jo and hate yourself. Your dad would not be happy to learn you were gay."

"Yeah, he wouldn't have been thrilled... Maybe I got lazy over the last three years."

"No, you got comfortable. Abby, don't let this town get its hooks into you. Digger's Cove is nice, but I wonder if it's you. But what do I know? I am just an ex-beauty queen. You got dinner plans?"

"The new guy in town offered me dinner but hasn't called."

"The new guy?"

"I think I was flirting just to annoy Paige."

"I thought she and the mayor were getting together."

"So did I?" Abby said, leaning back in her chair.

"So you're going to sit here..."

"Hell no," Abby said, standing up and gulping her coffee. "I need a shower. How about we meet at the diner?"

"How about you let me use your shower?" Allison May said. The house is locked up. All my stuff is packed. I am supposed to be on my way to New York."

"You can use my spare bedroom. It has a bathroom. I may as well put you up since I am making you stay here."

"You just want to keep an eye on me," Allison May said.

"You are spoiling the beauty queen stereotype."

"That we are all dumb?" she said, then flashed her million-watt smile.

"Exactly. Let's get out of here."

CHAPTER 34

"So basically, you got nothing," Allison May said as she picked up her wine and studied it. "Is this half full or half empty?"

"Half empty, which makes me a pessimist," Abby said, pushing away her plate. The only bit remaining of her cheeseburger was the pickles she had picked off. "As for my murders, I have nothing. I am still convinced if I knew why Jimmy was coming back, I'd know why he was murdered. It wasn't just to collect a reward. I am sure Sinclair would have been happy to wire him the money through Western Union. He had a notebook with five names on it. One of them yours."

"I told you, I really didn't know the guy," Allison said with a shrug. "It's a mystery to me."

"I got to ask you something," Abby said. "You had a medical procedure in L.A. I don't suppose you want to tell what it was?"

"I was really hoping you wouldn't find out about that," Allison said, slumping back in her seat. She swirled her wine around her glass. "But I guess you will find out anyway. I was attempting to fix something inside me. This perfect body is not so perfect. I can't have kids. Operation failed. I told you, things aren't settled with the lawyers. My lawyers tried to cut me out of my trust. They thought they were being pretty clever."

"Once again, underestimating you," Abby said, pouring herself some more wine.

Allison May gulped down her wine. "Greed makes people stupid. As I told you. It turns out that grandfather's being old-fashioned is illegal. You can no longer discriminate against the women in your family regarding inheritance. I learned that while getting my law degree. I confronted them with these facts when they told me there would be no more money. They told me they had to honor my grandfather's wishes. They were being pretty damn smug about it." Allison May leaned back in the booth, looking pretty smug. "It wasn't until I filed papers that they realized I was serious."

"Then suddenly they are kissing your ass," Abby said.

"Not at first. A lot of male posturing and, oh, Abby, you are being silly. Let's go back to the way it was. They assumed, like so many people, that I was just another dumb bimbo. Would be thrilled to get the crumbs they gave me. When they read my complaint, they realized I wasn't stupid and learned enough about the law to win my case. It might have taken me years, but I would have won."

"So they gave you the money," Abby said.

"A token sum. I am their biggest client. If I sued and won, they would be ruined. Not to mention, their reputations would be down the toilet. I know one thing: those New York lawyers have been ripping me off. I don't know how, but they are. They are acting like it is their money. The real reason I want to get out of town is that on Monday morning, their offices will be raided by the FBI. Who, it turned out, had suspicions about them? They just needed an excuse to go in. I gave it to them. I wanted to be there to see that. To see those smug assholes go down. I am hoping there will be blood on the walls. But I would settle for them being taken out in handcuffs. My new lawyers who specialize in this kind of thing will be there."

"I'm sorry, but it will be just two days," Abby said. Ah! Walt got a phone call from the FBI asking to be kept up on the progress of the case. One mystery solved."

"Who is the new guy with Megan?" Allison May asked, nodding toward the bar.

Abby saw Sam standing with a tall, voluptuous redhead dressed in a lovely white business suit with red trim. Her hair was pinned up into a simple twist. Sam said something that made her laugh and touch his arm. "His name is Sam. He owns the bike Jimmy was riding. He came here from Vegas. I think Sam is thinking of settling here. I thought he was a nice guy. He offered to buy me dinner."

"Now he is here with Megan," Allison said, leaning forward and pouring wine into her glass. "Isn't she a Baptist or something?"

"Conservative Baptist. Why?"

"Well, I am not the expert, but Megan is trying to get laid. Touching his arm, acting interested in every word he says, and giggling."

"So you really are..."

"Close, but not completely. It was painful for me. It's better after the operations, but I still can't have kids. Which is a little sad. There she goes, laughing again. Sam reminds me of someone. Maybe it's that actor who plays cowboys all the time."

Abby looked back and then returned her attention to Allison May. "Why am I annoyed? I am annoyed because I also made a fool of myself in front of Paige. Or is it just my ego? He's here with Megan and not me."

"Would you really want to be here with him?"

"No, I would rather be here with you."

"Or Merry Jo."

"Shut up."

"That's one of the reasons I am leaving. My doctors tell me sex will get better for me. There is a shortage of men in this town."

"Yes, there is..." Abby said, looking back. Now I don't see it."

"Seeing what?" Allison May asked.

"Seeing why I flirted with him."

"Stop it, Abby! You got two murders to solve and not a clue who did it."

"Yeah, two dead bodies do put crimp in your social life."

"Merry Jo is back in town." Allison May.

"Yes, and her name is on my list," Abby said, letting off a sigh and then gulping down her wine. I already talked to her. She called, and I still haven't called her back."

"Personal call?" Allison said. "Maybe she—"

"OH crap, Shaun told me it was about the murder. I better go talk to her."

"Don't take your gun. You might end up shooting your old friend. Not that it would be a bad thing. Merry Jo and I never got along... Speaking of the devil."

Merry Jo walked into the diner dressed in ripped jeans, a tank top, and a leather jacket. Her black hair looked like an angry mane around her beautiful face. She scanned the room, spotted Abby, and walked over. She nodded at Allison May. "I've been trying to call you."

"I have been busy," Abby said. "I have two murders."

"Now you got three," she snapped.

CHAPTER 35

"Okay, this is just getting ridiculous." Abby was looking down at the dead body lying in the doorway of Merry Jo's barn. There were three bullet holes in his chest. She squatted down and studied the wounds, sighing. "Well, Foster, you were a jerk but didn't deserve this. Why did you call early?"

"Someone called and told me it would be a real good idea if I went back to New York," Merry Jo said. "I thought it was because I'm gay, but then they said you might find your cute ass in jail for murder."

"When did you find him?"

"About an hour ago, just when I got back from Cornwall."

"You were in Cornwall all day? Who did you see?"

"Most of the day. The university is having a gay pride day. They wanted me to attend."

"All day? That shouldn't have taken all day," Abby said, standing up. Then smiled. "They wanted a free sculpture."

"Yes, they did. Were real pushy about it. I only took a few classes. It wasn't like I really attended college there. You think I did this?"

"I think someone wants me to think you did it. I have a feeling I am going to find the murder weapon around here someplace." She was looking over when Bruce and Lucy walked into the barn. "Thanks for coming in, Lucy. Phil is looking for a car. Foster didn't walk out here. Just take a quick look around the barn and outside. The state guys are on their way."

"Is that Foster?" Lucy asked.

"Yes, it is."

"The boy was a moron, but no reason to shoot him," Bruce said with a shake of his head. "You going to tell the mayor?"

"Of course, I will tell the mayor," Abby snapped. Merry Jo looked down

. "I am getting pissed. I am going to look around the house."

Merry Jo and Abby walked toward the house in silence until they reached the front door of her house.

"You don't think I did this, do you?" Merry Jo asked.

"No, but someone sure wants me to," Abby said, waiting for Merry Jo to open the door. Finally, she nodded toward the door. "You don't have to let me in. The crime scene is out in your barn. I can get a warrant."

Merry Jo shook her head, opened the door, and waved Abby in. The front room was nicely furnished with overstuffed furniture flor, all wallpaper, and several lovely paintings. Everything looked new and fresh. The Sheriff took it all in. "You really are staying. You got rid of all your old man's stuff."

"His macho dark wood and animal heads on the wall weren't me."

"I really like the wallpaper."

"Thank you. Brightens the place up."

"Your dad wasn't thrilled when you came out," Abby said, moving into the middle of the room and slowly turning. "Do the whole house?"

"Yes... Daddy only forgave me after I sold my first piece...the first piece that sold for half a mil and got me on the cover of PEOPLE."

"Money does change people." She looked down at the recliner and groaned. "You got to be kidding me. Do they think I am stupid?"

"What?" Merry Jo asked, rushing over to look down. "Is that a gun?"

They were both looking at the handle of a pistol sticking out of the side pocket of the chair. Merry Jo was shocked. Abby knelt down and glared at it. She looked pissed. "Sure, as there is a god, that is the gun that killed Lionel and Foster."

Walt walked in and joined them by the chair. "A gun."

"Yeah, you better get your people in here," Abby said, standing up and sighing. "It's the mayor's son. I'll tell him."

"This your house, miss?" Walt asked, looking at Merry Jo.

"Yes, it is," Merry Jo said with a nod.

"Well, I have a lot questions for you," Walt said. "You will have to..."

Abby was in his face before he could finish. "Don't you dare? She didn't do it."

"Abby, I have no choice..."

"The hell you don't. She didn't do it," Abby snarled. "This is a setup. Are you too stupid to see that?"

"Abby, I have no choice," Walt said, taking a step back, but Abby followed him. "I got a gun and a dead body. I gotta take her in...just for some questions."

"You take her in," Abby yelled. I will dump this case in your lap. I won't lift a finger to help, and when she is proven innocent, I will tell the world I told you so!"

"Abby, come on!"

"Abby," Merry Jo stepped up, turned the Sheriff around, and hugged her. "Calm down. I need you to stay on the case. You have to prove me innocent. You may be the only one who can."

"I can't let them take you in..." Abby said with almost a whimper.

"Yes, you can. I will be fine. I have you watching my back," Merry said, pulling away and smiling. Now get to work."

Abby hugged her and turned to Walt. "No handcuffs."

"There are no handcuffs, but it might be best you leave," he said. I will send you all the reports. I don't know what is going on here."

"I am leaving," Abby agreed. "My deputies stay. I am still on the case. I am going to find the son of bitch who did this. I am going to find them. Oh, you get to tell the mayor his son is dead."

Merry Jo hugged Abby again and smiled. "You go get them, girl."

CHAPTER 36

Abby stormed into the station. Shaun looked up and opened his mouth. She raised her hand without stopping. "Not now."

Paige stood but got the same response. She watched Abby get some coffee and head for her office. Finally, Paige says, "Abby."

"What?" she snaps, stopping and glaring at everyone.

"Walt dropped off the coroner's report, Jimmy's personal stuff, and Lionel's and Foster's personal effects. The gun you found in Merry Jo's house was the same one that killed Lionel and Foster. It's all on your desk."

"Thank you, give me a minute," Abby said and went into her office. She slumped into her chair and sipped her coffee. After a while, Abby opened the bottom drawer on her desk. She took out the old photo of her and Merry Jo, looking very happy. Abby stared at the picture, muttered a curse, put it back in the drawer, and slammed it closed. Only then did she notice the plastic bags on her desk and the stack of paper? She held them up one at a time. One contained some kind of medal. An odd-looking award of some sort. Another was a gold watch with what looked like diamonds. A wallet was in another bag. There was a list of contents taped to the bag. "Thirty dollars, a twenty, a five and five singles. Expired license. Bus ticket, book of stamps, and pawn ticket for a gold chain worth two hundred bucks."

She picked up more bags and stared at them. There was a set of keys in two different bags. Two bags contained pistols. A small notepad and pen were in the other one. She frowned, found some crime scene gloves, and pulled them on. She took out the notepad. It was almost new. Still stiff and shiny. On the first page were the five names. Each name had a number beside it. The rest of the pages were blank. "What the hell? Oh, Jimmy, why are you complicating my life? Why couldn't you get yourself killed somewhere else?"

Abby put the notepad back in the bag, picked up the report, and started to read. "Shot in the face. .22 caliber bullets."

She turned the page. "What the hell!"

Abby grabbed the phone and angrily punched in a number. She tapped her fingers on the desk while listening to the rings. Someone picked up.

"What the hell, Walt. You dump this report on my desk and just leave. You don't wait to discuss it!"

"Hello to you, too, Abby. I assumed you were still a little miffed at me," Walt said in a dry tone. "I'll have your friend home in two hours. The gun was wiped clean, and there were no powder burns on her or her clothes. Plus, I have other cases. A lot of other cases. I was going to come back."

"He had cancer!" Abby snapped, looking at the report. "Lung cancer. Stage four. The odds were, Jimmy was a dead man."

"So why kill him?"

"The killer probably didn't know," Abby's tone softened. "Sorry, Walt, we'll talk later. Thanks for...well, you know."

Abby hung up the phone before he could say goodbye and leaned back in her chair. For a long time, she stared at the ceiling. Suddenly, Abby sat up and grabbed the bag with the pen and notepad. She quickly looked through all the bags. She sat straight up, holding the bag with a set of keys. "Son of a bitch."

CHAPTER 37

Abby came out of her office and was about to say something when she noticed Nancy in jeans and a blouse standing by Shaun's computer, with Paige looking over their shoulders.

"What's going on?"

"It's the video from the road," Paige said. "Nancy says we have to see something. I would have knocked, but you were in a mood."

"Yeah, yeah," Abby said joining them by the computer. The screen showed an empty road. Jimmy rode up and skidded to a stop. He pulled off his helmet and smiled. The smile vanished just before he was shot. Lionel ran into the shot a second later and bent over the body. He was searching for it.

"Lionel did kill Jimmy," Paige said.

"I guess so," Abby said then frowned. She moved closer and pointed to the monitor. "Go back and zoom in on the corner. Right there."

"What did you see?" Shaun asked, typing away.

They watched the screen but only saw a black blur in the corner.

"What was that?'" Nancy asked.

"Shaun, can you do a frame-by-frame?" Abby asked.

"Oh please, ask me to do something difficult," Shaun said with a snort. He tapped the key over and over. "THERE!"

"A leather glove," Abby said. "Lionel was there, but he wasn't the killer. Run the rest."

They watched as Lionel jumped up and pointed. He ran out of the shot. A few seconds later, a car came up and stopped. The driver got out and stared down at the body.

"I don't think they found what they were looking for," Paige said.

"I think you're right," Abby said. She went back into the office and came out with the bags. She looked through them. What were they looking for?"

"Where did you get that?" Nancy asked, grabbing the plastic bag with the medal in it. "I thought Kirk lost this."

"What is it?" Abby asked.

"This is the actual medal from the TV show," Nancy said. "Not the one he wore, but the one he looked at in one episode. I think the one with plants."

"Is it valuable?" Abby asked.

"Oh yes, we have the documentation to prove its provenance. I am not sure the exact value..."

"Provenance...you need that to prove it is the real deal," Abby said, holding up the bags. "Or it is just another medal."

"Of course, there are probably hundreds of fakes out there," Shaun said.

"Fakes, fakes," Abby said, going over to Lucy's desk and dialing a number. "Nancy, do you have the paperwork here?"

"Of course not," Nancy said. "The family has it. If Kirk found it. It could hurt his therapy. Sheriff..."

Abby held up her hand. "Allison May, Abby here. Are you missing a Rolex?"

"No...oh, wait," Allison May said. "I have a real Rolex, but that is in a safety deposit box. I did have a replica. Who wears three hundred thousand dollars on their wrist? Turns out I was right. Someone stole it while I was in Vegas."

"I need you to come over and look at a watch we found on Jimmy."

"That son of bitch stole it. He must have been so disappointed when he found out it was only worth a hundred bucks."

"Exactly. Thanks. We will talk later." Abby hangs up the phone and looks at the bags again. The others watched her. Finally, she looked up. "I know why Jimmy was coming home."

CHAPTER 38

"You said once you knew why Jimmy was coming back to town," Paige said, "you would know who the murderer was. So who is it?"

"I figured, like everyone else, Jimmy was coming back to pull off some sort of scam," Abby said, holding up the bags. "But he wasn't. Jimmy was dying. He was coming back to make amends. He stole these, thinking he could sell them but couldn't. For some reason, he held on to them."

"Back up," Paige said. "Jimmy was dying?"

"Yes, he had lung cancer, fourth stage."

"Oooo, he always was a heavy smoker," Shaun said. "Those cancer sticks will catch up with you."

"So you're saying he was coming back to give those things back?" Paige said, nodding her head. "Trying to get right with God."

"Nothing like death to make you come home and make amends. The medal back to Kirk," Abby said. "Allison May gets her watch back. He bullied Keanu in school. Mocked Lizzie all the time. He wanted to apologize face to face. I am sorry for being a jerk."

"Lady Elizabeth," Shaun corrected her.

Abby ignored him. "He brought a notepad. I think he was making a list of people he had wronged."

"That would be the whole town," Shaun said with a shrug.

"That's why he wanted the reward money brought here. He was going to give it to his kid."

"Then why is he dead?" Shaun asked.

"Wait. Wait," Abby said, pacing around. She stopped, ran back into her office, and came out with Jimmy's wallet. She pulled it out of the bag, looked through it, and pulled out a bus ticket. "Ha! He had a bus ticket. Bus to come home. If he had the ticket, why did he steal the bike?"

"The bus is slow. A bike would be faster," Paige said.

"Yes! That's it," Abby laughed. "Something happened in Vegas to make Jimmy change his plans. He needed to get here as fast as he could. He just spent most of his money on a bus ticket. So he couldn't afford airfare."

"But what? What happened?" Shaun asked.

"I don't know..."Abby said, going to the coffee pot and pouring herself another cup. She stopped. "I need to know when he found out he was dying and when he contacted Sinclair. The cancer is what changed Jimmy. Before that, he was the old Jimmy."

"So Jimmy, being Jimmy, was probably trying to steal or run some scam to get himself some money. You think Lionel was in on it?"

"Yes, Lionel was probably thrilled to be in on it, but there is someone else. The killer," Abby said. "Jimmy and Lionel cooked up some kind of scam that the third guy thought was worth killing for."

"Whatever they were planning was going down here," Paige said. "Jimmy was coming here to stop it. Why's Lionel dead?"

"He was a witness. Yesterday, he chatted me up. He wanted to confess. I handled him all wrong. Should have been a good cop. If I listened, he might have told me everything."

"So, is the killer still here?" Shaun asked. "Maybe he left town."

"Maybe...unless he plans on trying to pull off the scam by himself," Abby said. "I have to find out what the scam was..."

"How are you going to do that?" Paige said.

CHAPTER 39

"I just need the date he found out he had cancer," Abby said into the phone, looking like she was about to explode. "I don't need a diagnosis or any medical stuff. Your patient was murdered...I just...Thank you!"

Abby hung up the phone and picked up the bus ticket. Shaun and Paige watched from the doorway. Abby smiled.

"What?" Paige asked.

"Jimmy found out he was dying two days after he brought the bus ticket and hocked the gold chain," Abby said with a smile. "He wasn't supposed to show up until today. He showed up almost two days early. My guess is Jimmy needed an alibi."

"So whatever scam Jimmy was pulling was supposed to happen on the day he died or yesterday," Paige said. "But nothing happened."

"Maybe Jimmy, showing up, stopped it," Abby said to herself. "No, the killer thought he could still pull it off, even with Jimmy dead. But then Lionel dies. Tying up loose ends. Eventually, Lionel would have talked. He just saw one of the few friends he had killed. What was he looking for?"

They all looked up when someone entered the station. Abby and the deputies met Sinclair, who was still looking quite English. "Sheriff, I got your message. How can I help you?"

"How many times did you talk to Jimmy Evans?" Abby asks.

"Three times," Sinclair said. "The first call was him telling us about Lady Elizabeth. Second, he confirmed he was right, as well as the reward. Then, the last one was setting up the meeting."

"Did you notice a change in attitude?" Abby asked.

"Not really...no. You're right. I could tell Mr. Evens was after money in the first two phone calls. During the last phone call, he seemed more concerned about Lady Elizabeth. Kept telling me to get here as quickly as possible..."

"Oh, my God. Jimmy was going to kill Lizzy!" Shaun gasped.

"Why would he want to kill Lady Elizabeth?" Paige asked.

"If Lizzie dies, Lionel will inherit," Abby said.

"That would be true, but I just received a phone call from my office," Sinclair said. "There may be a third heir."

"Who?" Abby asked. "Here in town?"

"We don't know. A possible cousin settled in Oregon. He was married, but there is no record of children. They died in a car accident. We are trying to get details. This was almost thirty years ago."

"Still, Jimmy didn't know about this third heir. He figured if Lionel inherited the title, he would be set for life," Page said.

"Jimmy was a lot of things but not a killer," Abby said. "Lionel definitely wasn't."

"So the third guy was hired to kill Lizzie. Killed them," Paige said. "Kills Lionel because he is a loose end. He's got to be long gone. No way would he stick around after two murders."

"Yeah," Abby muttered. "But this is Digger's Cove. We would have noticed a stranger in town."

"The only stranger in town is Sam."

"And he is from Vegas," Abby said. "So why the hell is he still here? Killing Lizzie does him no good."

"Maybe he likes it here?" Shaun said.

"Shaun, run a background check on Sam," Abby said. "Paige, there are only two ways in and out of this town. Car and bus. Check with Sid over at the bus station. I want to know when Sam got into town. It had to be by bus."

"We do have another visitor in town," Paige said.

CHAPTER 40

"Merry Jo?" Abby asked, looking at Paige.

"She is new in town," Paige said. "She has been gone for three years..."

"I know you don't like Merry Jo, but she is not a killer."

"All due respect, Sheriff, your judgment may be a little clouded when he comes to Merry Jo. We did find the murder weapon at her place and a dead body."

"She didn't do it. The state police had already let her go. My question is, how did an outsider know to frame Merry Jo?"

The two women stared tensely at each other. Shaun watched with big eyes.

"I know you don't like Merry Jo..."

"And everyone in town knows how you feel about her. I am suggesting you let me take over Foster's murder."

"You have a conflict there," Abby coolly said.

"What?" Paige said, sounding surprised.

"Foster drove out to Merry Jo's in the red Corvette using the keys. The keys that we all saw the mayor take off of him. How did Foster get the keys?"

The staring contest continued.

"Sheriff," Sinclair interrupted. "It sounds like Lady Elizabeth may be in some danger. I would like to arrange to move her out of town as soon as possible."

"That is a good idea," Abby said, pointing her finger at the man and nodding. "Get her out of town. Take her to New York. Stay there until we get this wrapped up."

"Thank you, Sheriff. It sounds like you have everything under control. I will let you know where we will stay in New York." Sinclair nodded and rushed out.

"With Lizzie out of town, that will take some of the pressure off. Okay, we focus on Sam. I want to know everything about him."

"I am off to the bus station," Paige said with a nod and headed for the door, but she stopped. "Abby, I am sorry, but it had to be said."

"Go." Abby sighed.

"Let's see what secrets our new guy is hiding," Shaun said, returning to his computer and typing.

"What am I missing?" Abby said, going to the coffee pot. "I heard something that just didn't register. What were you looking for, Lionel? You didn't find it. I should have it."

"Unless Jimmy hid it someplace for his protection. Maybe he knew he would be searched," Shaun said.

"Shaun, then he would have to know he was in danger. He knew at least one of them was a killer," Abby said, looking at her deputy. She started to drink her coffee but paused. "Jimmy was broke. He probably had no insurance. He was looking at a long, painful death. Did Jimmy commit suicide?"

"You mean like suicide by cop, but not a cop? He had the notebook and all that stuff."

"He knew his partners would kill him. Maybe he didn't expect to be killed right outside of town. Maybe Jimmy thought he had time. He knew we found all that stuff. Figured it out...but he took the trouble hiding something important to the killer. What did you hide, Jimmy? Where did you put it?"

"Abby, you all right?" Shaun asked.

"Call Lucy, I want to know where Sam Ellis is right now," Abby said.

Shaun nodded and turned to the radio. His phone rang. He quickly picked it up. "Digger's Cove Sheriff's Department."

He listened and looked at Abby. "I will get the sheriff right away."

"Who is it?" Abby asked.

"It's the FBI from New York."

CHAPTER 41

"Sheriff Anderson speaking, how can I help you?" Abby asked, standing by Paige's desk. She glanced down at the desk pad. It was covered with doodles of squares. That brought a smile to her lips but vanished with a male voice that spoke,

"Sheriff, I am Special Agent Nolan. I work out of the New York office. I have just come across some information that may be pertinent to a case you are working on. We are working with Allison May Town..."

"Oh yeah, the thing with her lawyers..."

"We were waiting for Miss Town to return to New York to raid their offices. She called yesterday and explained the situation, so we proceeded with the raid. During the raid, we discovered the firm had put a contract on Miss Town's life. We tried contacting her, but cell phones don't work in your town. We tried the landline, but there was no answer."

"She's staying at my house," Abby said and quickly gave him the number. Has anyone taken the contract? No, better question: Do you know the name Sam Ellis? He lives in Las Vegas."

"Not a Sam Ellis, but Sam Edwards. He works out of Vegas - or did. It appears he closed his body shop and sold his house."

"Tall guy with white hair and mustache?" Abby asked. "Looks like a cowboy from the movies?"

"That's Sam. If he is there, Sheriff, he is dangerous."

"He has a rifle with him. Said it was a Winchester."

"He has used a rifle, but his specialty is bombs."

"I have to go..."

"Sheriff, I'll contact our local office and get a couple agents sent out. Be careful."

"Thanks. I will take any help you can send," Abby said, hanging up the phone and opening her bottom drawer. She stared at the picture for a second, then grabbed a pistol in a holster. Abby pulled out the

Smith & Wesson M&P9 and checked it like a pro. After checking it, she slammed the mag back in, then moved out the door, pulling on the holster. "Call Paige, Lucy, and Phil and tell them to get to my house. Now!"

"You putting on your gun?" Shaun said, staring at his boss.

"Shaun, do it! Our guy might be after Allison May, so tell them to be careful!" Abby yelled, rushing out the door without waiting for an answer. She jumped into the car and pulled away from the curb. Her lights and siren were on before she reached the corner.

Abby lived less than ten blocks from the station, so it was a short, fast trip. She stopped up the street from her house and climbed out of her car, pulling her pistol at the same time. A few people came out of the houses to watch. Abby yelled, waving her pistol. "Get back in your houses! Get back inside!"

The people just stood there. Abby was tempted to shoot one for being so stupid.

"Abby, what are you doing?"

Abby whirled around and stared at Allison May, holding a paper shopping bag on the sideway. She grabbed her friend by the arm and pulled her behind the car. Allison dropped the bag, the glass breaking.

"Abby!" Allison gasped. "That was expensive wine!"

"Allison May, your New York lawyers put a contract on you."

"They want me dead?" she asked, looking genuinely surprised. "Wow, they must be really ripping me off. How did you know?"

"The FBI called me. Good news, I'm pretty sure I know who the killer is."

"Who?"

"Megan's new boyfriend," Abby said, peeking over the car. A second later, the antenna was shot off. She ducked down. Two more police cars raced onto the street. They blocked off the street. Lucy climbed out of one car. A tall, thin, balding man in a uniform climbed out holding a shotgun. Abby waved at them and motioned for them to go to the back of the house. She looked at Allison. "Stay here. I don't think he will take another shot."

"Stay here...alone?" Allison asked. "I don't think so. You got the gun. You got an extra gun?"

"Allison May—" Abby was cut off by four gunshots. "Crap! Stay here!"

Abby jumped up and charged across the street with her weapon aimed in front of her. She moved between two houses and into an alley. The Sheriff aimed her pistol around and spotted Paige standing up the alley with her pistol aimed in front of her. "Paige! PAIGE!"

Abby ran up to her deputy and stopped beside her. "You see him?"

"He made me shoot him," Paige said in a monotone voice. "I didn't want to, but he started to bring up his gun."

Abby looked where Paige was aiming. Sam was lying sprawled out on the ground. Four bullets in his chest. A rifle with a scope lying beside his hand. Abby pushed Paige's hand down and carefully took the pistol. She handed it to Lucy, who had just run up, then moved over to the body and kicked away the rifle. She glanced at the modern rifle and high-tech scope. "Winchester .73 my ass. Stupid."

"I got Phil blocking off the alley and calling Shaun. I figure we need the state police here," Lucy said, looking at Sam's body. "I thought he was a nice guy. Megan is going to be upset."

"I am upset," Abby snapped, putting her arm around Paige and leading her down the alley. "Secure the scene. I'll be back."

"Take care of Paige," Lucy yelled. "I got this."

CHAPTER 42

"She going to all right?" Abby asked the older man in the suit.

"She will be fine," he said. "I've given her a sedative. I'll take her home and make sure she lies down. I'll check on her later."

"Thanks, doc," Abby said. She watched the doctor walk over to a 1950 Buick Road Master. Paige was sitting in the front seat of the bright blue and white car. Lucy walked up and nodded.

"Walt is here with his crime scene people," she said, looking around. "Not that we need them."

"A man is dead. Paige shot him. We need them," Abby said, shaking her head. "This is a stupid crime. Sam didn't strike me as stupid. This is a small town. There is no place to run. He didn't have a car. After he shot Allison May, where was he going?"

"Maybe he has a car stashed?" Lucy asked.

"In this town? Any car newer than 1975 is going to stick out like a sore thumb."

"He was a mechanic. He could have hotwired almost any car in town."

"Yeah, but most people keep an eye on their cars," Abby said, leaning against her car. She glared at the people still standing outside their houses. "Look at them. Nothing goes on here without someone noticing."

"Except for two murders," Lucy said.

"You trying to be funny? You're not. For him to shoot Allison May, steal a car, and get out of town would be a hell of a trick."

"Like pulling a rabbit out of a hat."

"The rabbit isn't in the hat. It's called the art of distraction... Oh, Crap!"

CHAPTER 43

"Abby, I don't think you should be doing that," Lucy said, standing across the street and watching Abby try to look under a bright red 1959 Cadillac Coup De Ville. I mean, if you are right, which I don't think you are."

"I am just looking," Abby said. "I think I can see something."

"Well, don't touch it. Lady Elizabeth will be pissed if you blow up her car."

"If the car blows up, we won't be around to hear her complain."

"Yeah, right. Thanks for that image." Lucy stepped back but stopped when a black SUV pulled up and parked behind Abby's Chevy. Two clean-cut men in almost identical suits climbed out and walked over to Lucy. "FBI, we were told to come by you give a hand."

"What is she doing?" the other agent asked, looking over at Abby. "Boy, you got some sweet cars in this town."

"That's the sheriff. She thinks there might be a bomb under that car."

"That might not be wise for her to do," he said.

"Hey, preaching to the choir," Lucy said, returning her attention to Abby.

"Do you have the suspect in custody?" the first agent asked.

"One of our deputies shot him. He was trying to shoot Allison May. She's okay, but my boss has it in her head that there is a bomb here."

"I read the man's sheet. He was a bomber. Excuse me." He went back to the SUV. He reached inside and took out a small silver mirror on a pole. The agent walked over and held it out to Abby. "Sheriff, it will be easier with this."

"Oh, thank you," Abby said, taking the mirror and using it to look under the car. She smiled, rolled over, and stood up. "I think I found something. You're FBI. You know about bombs?"

"As a matter of fact, I do," he said and got on the ground, pushing the mirror under the car. "This would be a real tragedy. A beautiful car like this. Hello. This guy meant business. Nice big charge. Oh my, he's got another charge under the back seat. Makes sense. This Cadillac is built like a tank, so he wanted to be sure."

Abby helped the agent up. She brushed off his jacket. Lizzie and Sinclair came out.

Lizzie asked, "Can we leave now?"

"Not in this car," Abby said. She looked at the agent. "Let's say you found the bomb. That way, you get the credit and can bring in your bomb guys."

"You sure?" he asked.

"Trust me, agent, there is enough credit to go around for everyone in this mess."

"I gathered that," he said. "Who is this?"

Abby turned and watched Merry Jo storm up the street, but she stopped in front of Abby, putting her hands on her hips. "You're all right. I heard you got shot!"

"I didn't get shot. Someone shot at me, but I am okay. Really, I am." Abby sighed. "He missed. Need a new antenna. Look..."

"What?" Merry Jo asked. "I thought you were shot. That is all I need. I come back here, and we argue. Then last night...well. Then you almost get shot before we can work it out..."

Abby pulled Merry Jo into her arms and hugged her. "I am fine. Can we talk later? I'm a little busy. I'll come by the house."

"Should I get some wine?" Merry Jo asked, holding on to Abby.

"Maybe some steaks. You can cook, unlike me."

"You still haven't learned?" Merry Jo pulled back and looked Abby in the face. "What am I going to do with you?"

"Really, I'm fine, MJ. We will talk tonight."

"You just called me MJ," she said, pulling away and smiling. She looked over at the car. "Bomb in the car, huh? Wow, who would have thought stupid Jimmy Evans would cause all this trouble?"

"Well, it's not all been bad." She wiggled one of Merry Jo's fingers. "I got to work."

"See ya later, Sheriff," Merry Jo said, happily walking off.

Abby walked back to the agent and Lucy, who was smiling. "She is a friend."

"Oh yeah, I could see that," the agent said.

"Wait," Abby said. She turned and watched Merry Jo walk off. "MJ is right."

"About what?" Lucy asked.

"Jimmy was stupid."

"Yeah, we all know that," Lucy said.

"So how did stupid Jimmy Evans figure out Lizzie was Lady Elizabeth? It took the English lawyers longer than it took Jimmy."

"How did he know?" Lucy said, nodding her head. "Jimmy could barely read. I can't see him doing some serious research. Oh no, Abby, we got the guy. It's over. Right? It's over. Let it go."

"I can't...we got another player out there. The one who has been pulling the strings all along," Abby said. She paused to think. "Lucy, have you ever seen the old movie Easy Rider?"

"Is that one with the hippies on the motorcycles?"

"Great movie," one of the agents said. "I thought Dennis Hopper had the cooler bike."

"You remember where they hide the drug money?"

CHAPTER 44

"My shift just ended," Lucy said.

"Put in for overtime," Abby said as she unlocked the door to a metal shack behind the station. She yanked the door open and stepped in. Jimmy's bike, covered with plastic, sat in the middle of the shed. Abby walked over to the bike and yanked off the plastic. She took the cap off the gas tank and peered in with a flashlight. "It's empty," she said.

"Maybe the lab guys already looked," Lucy said. "Can we go now?"

"I was sure I was right," Abby said, looking disappointed. She looked at Lucy and shrugged. "Go home."

"I am still putting in for overtime. Abby, it's over. We can all go back to being bored."

"Yeah, night, Lucy."

CHAPTER 45

Abby sat at her desk, staring at the plastic bags. Then, she picked them one at a time. She rolled the bag, holding the wallet in her hand. "You had something they wanted. What did you have? Sure, as there is a God, someone else is behind all this. Sam came to town to kill Lizzie and Allison May. Was he just being greedy? Jimmy somehow finds out Lizzie is the heir to a fortune. He also finds out Lionel is in line right after Lizzie. So he decides to kill Lizzie. Lionel inherits. He's rich. Then Jimmy finds out he is dying. All the money in the world won't save him. He comes home to make amends and save Lizzie. Gets killed even before he reaches town. What are the odds of Jimmy and those New York lawyers hiring the same hitman?"

Abby stood up and stretched. The phone rang. She snatched it up. "Sheriff's office."

"You still there?" Merry Jo asked. "The steaks and wine are in the fridge. Get your ass over here."

"I am coming. I just need to go home, shower, and change."

"You can shower here. Scrub your back...sorry, I am moving too fast."

"No, no...actually, that sounds great," Abby said, picking up an envelope and reading the label. Then she pulled it closer. "Son of a bitch."

"That's rude, or are you going to be late?"

"Stamps. Jimmy had stamps."

"What?"

"I am going to be a little late...no, wait."

CHAPTER 46

Abby sat in the dimly lit kitchen. She studied some documents, looking very sad. A bump made her look up. Another bump made her let off a sigh. "They're in here."

Abby stayed seated at the table as someone stepped into the kitchen. "I was hoping you wouldn't show up," she said. "But here you are. With a gun. Another pistol? How many do you guys have?"

"Dad's collection. Not all of them were registered," Paige said, bringing up the snub nose .38. "You took my weapon, but this will do."

"Department policy. An officer's weapon is always taken after a shooting. Please tell me Shaun isn't involved."

"Shaun? You're joking. He is too honest, but he did a lot of the research. Being adopted, I was curious about my real family."

"He didn't make the connection," Abby said. "But you did. According to this, you and Lizzie are half-sisters. I wonder how that happened. Well, small town. The same guy gets two women knocked up. One he marries, and the other leaves town. Puts you up for adoption. You end up back here."

"Lizzie always told me she loved me like a sister. A younger sister."

"She was born first. She wins the lottery. I am sure Lizzy would have taken care of you."

"Yes, my lady. No, my lady. Yes, I am the bastard sister of Lady Elizabeth. No, thank you."

"You couldn't approach the English lawyers, claiming to be an heir after Lizzie dies. You become a suspect. You needed someone to approach the lawyers. Someone I would believe was the murderer after Lizzie turns up dead. Jimmy was going to be the fall guy. He didn't know about the bomb. Shows up. Boom. I arrest him."

"It was all supposed to be so simple."

"Why drag Lionel into it? You were next in line."

"That was Jimmy's doing," Paige said, stepping closer and aiming the pistol. "But I counted on that. Jimmy figured he could get a lot more if Lionel inherited. Jimmy gets his friend to kill Lizzie."

"Sam was already coming here to kill Allison May. What are the odds?"

"No idea. Obviously, Sam didn't know about me. He thought he was just going kill Lizzie and Allison May, then leave town. My guess is Jimmy planned on killing me."

"But you would kill him in self-defense. Then act surprised when it turned out you were royalty. We wouldn't believe anything Lionel said, him being the town nut."

"It was all so simple. Then Jimmy gets cancer. He had all those documents. You were supposed to find them on his dead body. The problem wasn't showing up early. It's who he might have talked to. I couldn't take the chance that he would come straight to you."

"Lionel knew Jimmy was coming early. Did he tell you, or did you follow him?"

"I led him to believe if he let me talk to Jimmy before he got to town, I would let him more than look at my tits."

"Jimmy stops when he sees Lionel. You shoot him. Somehow convince Lionel to keep his mouth shut."

"A few kisses and letting him cop a feel, and he was mine. I was terrified when I heard he was talking to you. I had no interest in sleeping with Lionel, so it was just easier to kill him."

"Heard? So our mayor was in on it, too," Abby said with a shake of her head. I found out the divorce was not that amicable? His wife cleaned him out. I assume Foster stumbled onto the plan and had to go. The mistakes were trying to frame MJ and giving Foster the car keys. You should have let him hotwire it. How did you get him to go out there?"

"I pretended I was Merry Jo. He was so stupid he believed."

"Instead of going to the bus station, you made sure that Sam planted the bomb. You saved Allison May by killing him and making yourself the hero. Case closed."

"How the hell did you figure out there was a bomb in Lizzie's car?"

"You didn't know the FBI called. They told me he was a bomber. I figured he was using the bomb as a distraction to get out of town after he killed Allison. Everyone is watching the burning car. Sam was a mechanic, so hotwiring a car would have been a snap...especially in this town."

"I guess Walt was right. You are good at this. Now give me those papers."

"James and Lisa already saw them. You going to kill them too?" Abby asked. "Where does it end, Paige? Was David long for this world?"

"Just give me the papers," Paige snapped and raised the gun. Suddenly, Merry Jo is behind Paige and has a Colt .45-six shooter pressed against her head.

"Why don't you give me that tiny pistol," Merry Jo said, "or I will use my huge gun to blow your head off. You know I don't like you, bitch."

"You heard the lady," Lucy said, stepping into the kitchen behind Abby. Her pistol was aimed at Paige, too.

"We got it all recorded," Walt said, coming up behind Lucy.

"It's over," Abby said, standing up and holding her hand. "Please."

"I really wasn't going to kill you," Paige said, handing Abby the pistol.

"I don't get to shoot her?" Merry Jo said.

"Not today. Maybe for your birthday. Walt, read this bitch her rights. I need some air."

CHAPTER 47

"Lady Elizabeth has left town," Lucy said, standing by the coffee pot. She sipped her coffee and took a cookie from the plate. "So has Allison May, but the FOR SALE sign in front of her house is gone. She may be coming back. Walt has taken Paige back to his headquarters..."

"Shaun, you okay?" Abby asked, leaning against a desk. "You want some time off?"

"I just started, Abby," Shaun said, looking up from his computer. "I always knew she was bitch, but wow. No, I would rather work than mope around the house. Any word on the mayor?"

"As I was saying, our mayor was picked up trying to cross the border into Canada. He will join Paige..., but probably not in the same cell. Our little town is back to normal," Lucy said.

"You want to be Head Deputy?" Abby asked Lucy.

"If I say yes, will I get a raise?"

"Yes."

"As the new Head Deputy, I suggest we hire another deputy to take my place. My cousin just moved here. She needs a job. She has a degree in English but worked as a security guard."

"Sounds like she is overqualified. Have her come in. I will talk to her."

Merry Jo poked her head in the door and asked, "You ready? Oh, cookies!"

She came over, picked one up, and took a bite. "Peanut butter, chocolate, and caramel?"

"Sea salt caramel," Shaun said with a smug smile. "I got the recipe from a murder mystery series I'm reading."

"Yum," Merry Jo said.

"Let's go. I only got an hour for lunch," Abby said, taking Merry Jo's elbow. "Lucy, you are in charge."

"Take your time," Lucy said. "I got cookies and need to move my stuff into Paige's desk."

Abby and Merry Jo came out of the station and walked down the street. "I am thinking of the deli."

"Yuck, pastrami with catsup," Merry Jo groaned.

"I don't like mustard and pickles. What is the big deal?"

"The big deal, Sheriff," Merry Jo said with a big smile, "We are walking down Main Street, and you are holding my hand."